Tailored and Veiled

A Delightfully Dysfunctional Familial Wedding

The Delightfully Dysfunctional Series Book #4

A Novel

Tiffany Ryan

Ebook: 979-8-9886983-6-4

Print: 979-8-9886983-7-1

This book is dedicated to my daughter, McKenna.

I am in awe of the woman you've become.

Chapter One

"Are you seriously going to make me do this every day for two whole weeks?" whined Beau. "It's my summer, Mom. I'm supposed to be free from anything that educates me."

"Well, you should have thought about that before wagering that ridiculous bet," said Mom, dicing a small green bell pepper. "And it's not like it's a full day of school, Beau. It's going over geography for ten minutes, so I think you'll live."

"Yes, but at what cost?" he countered. "That's 140 minutes of my summer that I will never get back. These are supposed to be the glory days of my youth, and now those moments are being stolen from me in ten-minute increments." He watched as Mom added the diced green pepper to a large bowl. "Besides, how was I supposed to know that you were some sort of Skee-ball wizard; you're old and enjoy reading and putting jigsaw puzzles together; you're not exactly someone who frequents arcades."

"Call me old again, and we'll make it three weeks rather than two," said Mom, holding up the knife.

Last weekend, Mom accompanied Beau to his friend's birthday party at a local bowling alley. Just as the party was coming to a close, he decided to challenge her to a game of Skee-ball. To make things a little more interesting, he offered up a little wager whereby the loser would have to spend ten minutes every day for the next two weeks doing whatever the winner wanted. Unfortunately for Beau, he ended up learning the hard way that Mom will never accept a challenge that she can't win. So, it was honestly no surprise to any of us when he came back home with his tail tucked between his legs complaining that Mom had, and I quote, "swindled him mercilessly and taken advantage of his innocence."

"Actually, dork, that's exactly what should have alerted you," I said, grabbing a bottle of water from the refrigerator.

"Can we please refrain from the name-calling?" asked Mom. She looked over at Beau. "I think what your sister means is that Skee-ball has been around for a long time, and since I've been playing it since I was your age, it's really no surprise that I would beat you." She cracked open two eggs and added them to the bowl. "And I suppose the fact that I was one of the local Skee-ball champions back in the day probably didn't hurt either."

"Yeah, looking back on it, that probably would've been good information to have," he said irritably.

"Hey honey, did you already transfer my expenses from last week?" said Dad popping his head around the corner.

"Oh crap, I completely forgot to tell you," she said. "I'm so sorry!"

"No worries," he smiled. "I just wanted to make sure before I asked Tina where they were." He walked over and kissed her on the cheek, "So, what's for dinner?"

"Meatloaf, mashed potatoes, and butterbeans," she answered. "It's a new recipe I've decided to try and includes sour cream, which will hopefully keep it moist."

"Mmm, sounds delicious," he said. "But then again, everything you make is always wonderful."

"Ugh, speak for yourself," muttered Beau, rolling his eyes. He watched Dad walk back to his office and then asked, "Can I please be done now?"

"Let's do one more," she said, taking off her rings and laying them on the counter. "Show me where Massachusetts is and name the capital."

"Oh, that's an easy one; it's right here," he said pointing at the oversized wall map. "And the capital is Columbus."

"The location's correct, but the capital is actually Boston," she said as she started mixing the ingredients in the bowl.

"Well, at least I was close," he shrugged.

"Please explain to me how Columbus is even remotely similar to Boston," she said. "They're entirely different cities."

"Oh, you know, just switch a few letters around and you'll get the gist of what I'm saying."

"I don't think anyone with half a brain in their head will ever get the gist of what you're saying," I snarked.

"Well, that's unfortunate," he deadpanned.

As Mom continued mixing the meatloaf, her cellphone began to ring.

"Beau, would you mind answering that and putting it on speaker," she said.

"It's Ezra," he said, placing it on the counter next to her. "You know, you may want to warn him about dinner so he can make the necessary mental preparations; not everyone in this family shares Dad's bland palate."

"Keep that attitude up and I may just stop making you dinner altogether," she said.

"Promise?" he grinned.

"Just swipe and answer the phone, please," she glared at him.

"Hi Ezra," he answered congenially. "Mom's busy mixing up a big bowl of her famous meatloaf, so she's asked me to put you on speaker."

"Hi honey," she called out.

"Oh my gosh, Mom, you are never going to believe what just happened!" exclaimed Ezra.

"Did you not hear what I just said," beseeched Beau. "We're having meatloaf for dinner."

"No, I heard you," he said. "I'm just trying to keep that unpleasantness out of my head for the moment."

"Okay, that's enough about the meatloaf," snapped Mom irritably. She lowered her voice and then calmly said, "Ezra, honey, tell me what happened."

"I still can't believe it, but someone literally just called 911 on me," he said.

"What?" she shrieked. "Oh my God, Ezra, are you okay?"

"I'm fine Mom, really," he said. "It's actually a pretty funny story."

She immediately stopped what she was doing and asked warily, "Is this something I really want to know?"

"It's fine Mom, really," he soothed. "You just have to hear me out, okay?"

"Okay, fine, tell me what happened," she said.

"Well, I was driving home from work and started getting a little drowsy, so I pulled into a shopping center and parked under a tree so that I could take a quick nap. Anyway, I tried to lay back in my seat, but with me being so tall, it was hard for me to get comfortable, so I just decided to roll down my window and hunch forward so that I could lay my head and arms on top of the door."

"I'm sorry, are you telling me that hanging out the window is more comfortable than laying back in your seat?" asked Mom.

"It's actually quite a bit more comfortable," he said. "In fact, I think it really stretches out my back and helps me—"

"Ezra, focus," interjected Mom. "I need you to stay on topic."

"Oh yeah, sorry," he laughed. "Well apparently, this woman saw me hanging out the window and was worried that I had either been shot or had overdosed on drugs so she immediately called 911."

"Oh, dear God," muttered Mom, closing her eyes.

"I know, it's crazy, right?" he said. "Anyway, once they realized I was okay and not actually dead, they left."

"They just left?" she said. "They didn't do or say anything else?"

"I think the fire truck decided to drive over to Publix and do their grocery shopping. I mean they're already there, so it makes sense."

"Okay, well, if that was the worst thing that happened, then I suppose you can chalk this up to a lesson learned." She placed her hands back in the bowl and began to mix. "But Ezra, you really need to—"

"Wait, I'm not finished," he interrupted.

"Oh man, this is going to be good," snickered Beau. "I knew there had to be more."

Mom glared over at Beau and then looked back down at her phone. "Ezra, please tell me you didn't do anything stupid."

"I didn't do anything, Mom, I swear," he said defensively. "Why do you always automatically assume that I've done something wrong?"

"I'm a mother, it's what we do," she said.

"Mom, just let him tell his story," I said, taking the carton of eggs and putting them back in the refrigerator.

"Okay, fine," she shrugged. "What happened next?"

"Well, like I said, the fire truck was able to leave the scene without any issue at all, but the ambulance decided to take a shortcut through the dry cleaners' drive-thru and ended up hitting the awning above, so the entire canopy collapsed onto their vehicle."

"Oh my gosh, that is classic!" guffawed Beau. "Please tell me you recorded this."

"This can't possibly be my life," whispered Mom.

"Anyway, I ran over to see if everyone was okay or needed any help, but they said they were fine, so I just went back to my car," said Ezra. "You know, I actually feel kind of bad about it, but there really wasn't anything I could do."

"Were they mad at you for what happened?" I asked. "Did they try to blame you?"

"No, they were actually pretty cool about it, although the driver did give me a few dirty looks."

"Okay, well, what's done is done, I suppose," said Mom, taking a deep breath. "I'm just glad you're safe."

She turned on the faucet and rinsed her hands. "But please, Ezra, going forward, keep your head and all of your limbs inside your vehicle. I'd really rather this not happen again."

"So, do you think the driver's going to have to pay for the damages?" asked Beau.

"No, honey, taxpayers do," said Mom.

"What?" he screeched.

"Damages are covered in the yearly budget and come from city taxes, so yes, we end up paying for it," said Mom.

"Wait a minute, you're telling me that this guy did something stupid, and our hard-earned money is going to have to pay for it?" he asked indignantly. "Ugh, the government's always after their pound of flesh; it makes me sick."

"Okay, you really need to stop spending so much time with your father. You're beginning to sound just like him." She turned her attention back over to Ezra. "Honey, are you planning on coming home for dinner?"

"That depends, are we still having meatloaf?"

"Well, I'm not stopping now, so yes, we are," she said.

"Save yourself, Ezra!" yelled Beau as he ran up the back stairs. "Believe, me you don't want any part of this!"

"Actually, I think I'm just going to swing by Sabrina's house and surprise her with some Chinese takeout," said Ezra.

"You've spent an entire day working in people's yards in 90-degree heat. Don't you think you should shower first?" asked Mom.

"Nah, I'll just take a hoe bath in the car," he said dismissively.

"A what?" asked Mom.

"Hey, that's Sabrina on the other line," he said without answering the question. "I love you and please be sure not to save any meatloaf for me."

Mom stared down at the phone and then looked over at me. "What exactly is a hoe bath?"

"It's basically where you wipe yourself off with a bunch of baby wipes in lieu of taking a shower," I said. "It's kind of like a lazy man's shower, or at least that's what Beau likes to call it."

"How does Beau even know what a hoe bath is?" She pulled a baking dish out from under the counter. "You know what, on second thought, don't answer. I don't really think I want to know."

As Mom began pouring the meatloaf mixture into the baking dish, Grandma Helen breezed in through the back door. "Hello, my darlings!"

"Hi Grandma," I said. "I'm surprised to see you here; I thought you were starting rehearsals for *The Sound of Music* tonight."

"I still am, dear, but I needed to ask your mother—" She paused midway through her sentence and then said, "Oh, dear God, what is that disgusting monstrosity you're currently molding?"

"It's meatloaf," said Mom, patting the meat into a loaf. "And before you say it, don't. I've already caught enough grief over this from Beau and Ezra and I really don't need you adding your two cents as well."

"Darling, you have Italian blood running through your veins. Why would you ever willingly succumb to making a loaf of meat for dinner when you could be making fresh pasta and sauces? Did you learn nothing during our time in Italy?" She pointed at the oversized clump of meat resting in the dish. "Your ancestors would be appalled; I hope you know that."

"Did you come here to ask me something, Mother, or are you just going to continue standing there berating me over what you consider to be poor dinner choices?"

"Oh, calm down, Olivia," she rolled her eyes. "You're always so sensitive whenever it comes to your cooking."

"Gee, I wonder why," she pondered aloud.

Mom washed her hands again and placed the baking dish in the oven. "What's your question, Mother?"

"Oh, yes, that's right," she said, snapping her fingers. "Are we still planning on having that dinner with the Caudill's tomorrow?"

"You know perfectly well that their last name is Caldwell," said Mom. "And yes, we are."

Tim and Nancy Caldwell are the parents of my Aunt Christine's fiancée, Brian. Last Christmas, the two of them became engaged and the wedding planning was placed on hold until we came back from our family vacation in Italy. We've been back for a few weeks now, so Aunt Christine and Brian have finally decided to get the two families together for the first time (although they are both incredibly nervous about how well Nancy and Grandma Helen will actually get along). From what I understand they are two peas in a pod and Aunt Christine is worried that there will be a lot of tension in the air, especially since Nancy has recently expressed a desire to be included in the wedding planning.

"I'm sorry, but I cannot believe that woman had the audacity to hone in on my territory," she huffed. "I am the mother-of-the-bride, and I am the one who is supposed to be helping Christine plan her perfect day."

"Which is pretty much code for making it all about you," muttered Mom.

"I heard that, dear," she snarled, arching her brow. "Anyway, I need to make sure that I look absolutely stunning tomorrow so that I can prove to her that she cannot hold a candle to my elegance and grace."

"You've never even met the woman, Grandma. How do you know she wants to take over everything?" I asked.

"Because that's exactly what she would do if the roles were reversed," said Mom. "You know, you're not being entirely subtle about this, Mother."

"Subtlety is for recreants, my darling." She immediately turned on her heel and walked toward the back door, "And I'll be damned if I let this tawdry, self-serving mother of the groom take away my spotlight!"

Mom watched Grandma Helen stride confidently to her car and then let out a long breath. "God help us all, Addie, this is going to be one hell of a ride."

Chapter Two

"She seriously called her tawdry and self-serving?" asked Aunt Christine. "Please tell me you're joking."

"I never joke about what our mother says," said Mom, sipping her coffee. "It's usually so outlandish I've learned not to."

"She's never even met Nancy. How can she make that kind of assumption?"

"Chrissy, the woman thrives on attention and denigrates anyone who tries to steal her spotlight; this can't possibly come as a surprise to you," said Mom. "The moment Nancy asked to be included in the planning is the exact moment she became enemy number one; you have to know that."

"I guess I was just hoping she'd make an exception since this is supposed to be about Brian and me," she sighed.

Mom opened a box of coffee cake that was sitting on the counter and began cutting it into slices. "I hate to tell you this, dear sister, but the minute Brian proposed to you, it immediately stopped being about either one of you and became solely about her."

"Why would she think like that?" I asked, confused. "Everyone knows that weddings are about the bride and groom."

"You still have so much to learn about your grandmother, Addie," laughed Mom as she handed me a slice of cake. "That woman would milk the attention out of a cow if she thought it might actually work." Mom handed Aunt Christine a slice and then plated one for herself. "Your aunt's nuptials are simply going to be another stage on which she can perform."

"Ugh, this is going to be a nightmare, I just know it," lamented Aunt Christine, her hands cradling her head.

"Listen, I know Mom can be a lot to handle, but if the three of us work together, I think we'll be able to keep her in check," said Mom. "We just need to stay diligent and on top of things."

"I don't know, maybe Brian and I should just elope and call it a day; it may be easier in the long run," she said. "You know, we've actually toyed with the idea, but between Nancy and Mom, we know we'd never get away with it."

"You will do no such thing!" exclaimed Mom. "That is absurd thinking, and you know it."

"Careful now," snickered Aunt Christine. "You're starting to sound an awful lot like Mom." She slowly sipped her coffee. "No, we're not going to elope, although we're both beginning to wish we had. Planning a wedding is a lot of work, and now with Mom and Nancy in tow, I think it's going to be more work than it's worth."

"I understand where you're coming from, believe me," said Mom. "But this is Brian's first wedding, and even though it's your second, you never really had the opportunity to plan the first because Jack stole that from you when he whisked you away to Aruba, remember?"

"How could I not?" she answered. "I've never seen Mom so angry in my life; you know how much she hates anything tropical."

"Exactly," agreed Mom. "Listen, this is meant to be a special time in your life. You're marrying the man of your dreams and will be starting a wonderful life together. Don't let Mom or Nancy get in the way of you enjoying this time. You're going to make a beautiful bride, and your wedding is going to be exactly what you want it to be, I promise."

"Thanks, Ollie," she smiled, glancing at the clock. "Oh crap, it's later than I thought. I'm going to be late for my appointment with the wedding planner."

"You hired a wedding planner?" asked Mom.

"I did, yes," she said, grabbing her keys. "I'm hoping he'll be able to help run interference." She downed the rest of her coffee. "Lord knows between Mom and Nancy; we're going to need it."

Mom reached over and picked up Aunt Christine's plate. "Go, I've got this."

"Thanks," she said, heading toward the back door. "Don't forget, dinner's at 7:00."

"Okay, well, pregame is at 5:30 if you'd like to join us," called out Mom.

Aunt Christine stopped halfway through the door. "Pregame?"

"You don't expect to go to this thing sober, do you?" she asked.

"Good thinking, I'll see you at 5:30," she said.

"Wow, I can't believe they were actually contemplating eloping," I said. "Do you really think that Nancy and Grandma are going to make things that unbearable?"

"Not if I have anything to say about it," said Mom. "I refuse to let them ruin this for her."

"Ooh, coffee cake!" exclaimed Beau, coming up behind her. He lifted the lid and inhaled deeply. "And it's raspberry, my favorite."

"Oh no you don't," said Mom, taking the coffee cake away from him. "Have you seen the mess you left on the couch? You know, Beau, if you're going to continue to do what I specifically tell you not to do, you could at least stop leaving behind evidence that proves you're doing exactly what I have been telling you not to do."

"I'm sorry, could you please say that again, but in English this time?" he deadpanned.

"I'm serious, Beau, if you don't stop eating in the living room, I'm going to start charging you twenty dollars every time you do." She walked into the living room and pointed down at the couch. "And the price will go up with each infraction."

"Are you serious? Why would you do that?" he asked, his voice going up an octave.

"Because I'm tired of being ignored," she answered plainly. "You obviously don't care about following the rules in this house, so maybe having to pay for your obstinacy is the best way to move forward." She walked back into the kitchen and refilled her coffee cup. "And if that doesn't work, we'll move on to Plan B, where I make you spend one hour a night watching *Gilmore Girls* with me, and I don't even like that show."

"What?" he erupted in horror. "I can't believe you'd do that to me."

"Believe it," she said, pouring cream into her coffee. "Now, go and clean up that mess, and then you may have some coffee cake."

"Ugh, fine," he said defeatedly.

"And don't use Churchill as a vacuum cleaner this time," she called out after him. "He leaves drool all over everything."

"Aww man, that's not as much fun," he pouted.

"I tell you what, you clean up that mess, and I'll heat up a piece of coffee cake with some butter on it. How does that sound?" she asked.

"Like a bribe," he said. "Which I'm not above taking."

He walked over to Churchill and petted his head softly. "Sorry buddy, the warden is on the warpath, so we need to lay low for a while."

"Careful, Beau, I can just as easily heat this up for myself," warned Mom as she slathered butter on top of the cake and placed it in the microwave. She then turned her attention over to me. "So, Addie, are you getting excited about starting college in the fall? I still can't believe you won't be here every day; I'm going to miss you so much!"

For those of you who don't know, I recently graduated from high school and will be starting as a freshman at Kennesaw State University, which is located thirty minutes outside of my hometown in Canton, Georgia. I was blessed to receive both an academic and soccer scholarship that will more than cover the next four years of my education, but lately, I've been experiencing doubts about whether or not I want to continue with soccer. It's not that I don't love the sport, because I do; it's just that I feel in my heart it's time to move on and focus solely on my education. And rather than tell my parents, who have invested so much time and money over the years, I just keep silent, praying that this feeling will go away.

The only person in my family who knows any of this is Grandma Helen, and that happened strictly by accident when she overheard me discussing it with my best friend, Skylar. Surprisingly, she has been incredibly supportive and has encouraged me to tell my parents, but I just can't bring myself to do it for fear of what they may say. I don't want to disappoint them or have them hate me for making such a big change in my life, so I've just avoided talking about it altogether until I can figure out what I want to do.

"Yeah, well, speak for yourself," said Beau, sidling up next to me. "I for one, am literally counting down the days."

"Shut up, dork," I hissed.

"Beau, not everyone appreciates your humor, so please just eat your breakfast and keep your thoughts to yourself," said Mom.

"Who said I was joking?" he countered.

"For the love of everything that is holy, please tell me that you have coffee and that it has been brewed!" exclaimed Grandma Helen, bursting through the back door. "Your father drank the last of ours, and I could just kill him for not saving me any."

Mom reached for a mug, filled it with coffee, and handed it to her. "The man cooks, cleans, and does all of the grocery shopping, Mother; I think you may want to give him some grace."

"He also puts up with your schizophrenic kind of crazy, so I'd say he's more than earned that last cup of coffee," mumbled Beau.

Mom glared over at Beau and then returned her attention to Grandma Helen. "Listen, Mom, I'm glad you're here. I need to talk to you about something." She opened the refrigerator and pulled out the cream. "Tonight is a very important night for both Brian and Christine, so I really need you to promise me that you're going to play nice and not cause any trouble with Nancy."

"Oh please, I have absolutely no intention of causing a scene, darling," she said, pouring cream into her coffee. "I'm perfectly willing to let bygones be bygones as long as she understands that I, being the mother-of-the-bride, have more of a say than she does."

"This isn't a competition, Mother," said Mom. "The woman simply wants to have a part in some of the wedding planning; she's not trying to replace you." She placed the cream back in the refrigerator. "You have to remember that this isn't just Chrissy's wedding; it's Brian's as well. His family has just as much of a right to be a part of this as we do."

"My God, Olivia, you make me sound as if I'm some sort of tyrant," she said.

"Well, if the shoe fits…" said Beau, stuffing the last bite of coffee cake into his mouth.

"You're not a tyrant," said Mom. "You just have a tendency to be a little unyielding when it comes to things like this, that's all."

"As long as this Nancy person understands her place and doesn't try to weasel her way into where she doesn't belong, everything will work out perfectly," she smiled.

"Okay, well, I suppose I have no choice but to take you at your word," said Mom.

"You may want to think twice about that," muttered Beau.

"Stop," mouthed Mom.

"So, tell me, what's on everyone's agenda for the day?" asked Grandma Helen.

"Well, Beau and I are about to go upstairs so he can clean out the last three weeks of cleaning up his room he's stuffed under his bed," said Mom. "And then…"

"What?" interrupted Beau. "You didn't tell me we were doing that."

"Surprise!" she yelled excitedly. "I thought this would be the perfect way to spend my ten minutes."

"Hey, that's not how this is supposed to work," said Beau.

"I get ten minutes a day to do what I want, and this is what I want to do." She gestured toward a drawer before making her way up the back stairs. "Be sure to grab a few trash bags before you come up."

"Ugh, fine," he said, slowly walking over to the drawer with the trash bags. He grabbed a few and then reluctantly trudged up behind her, calling out, "A little heads-up would've been nice, you know. Now I have to realign my entire schedule. Those video games aren't going to play themselves."

"What in the world was that about?" asked Grandma Helen.

"Beau lost a bet to Mom playing Skee-ball and now whines like a baby any time she tries to collect," I said. "It's actually somewhat entertaining to watch."

"Well, stupid is as stupid does, I suppose," she sighed. "Which reminds me, have you spoken to your parents about quitting soccer?"

"It's not stupid, Grandma," I said curtly. "And no, I haven't."

"I'm not saying that quitting soccer is stupid, darling," she said. "I'm saying that not discussing it with your parents is." She quietly sipped her coffee and then added, "Personally, I can't stand the sport. I mean, all of that running around just to kick a ball into a box seems so inane and unimaginative to me. No, I much prefer figure skating; it's exciting, graceful, there's music, and more importantly, it takes place indoors."

"Yes, you've been telling me that for years," I said, rinsing my plate in the sink. "Seriously though, I don't even know how or where to start the conversation. They've both given so much of their time and money over the years that I'm scared they'll hate me if I stop playing. They're so proud of me for getting that scholarship."

"You know, I honestly don't think you're giving your parents enough credit, dear," she said. "Will it be a difficult conversation? Yes, I'm not saying that it won't. But you also have to understand that your happiness and peace of mind are more important to them than whether or not you choose to play collegiate soccer."

"I know, but what about the scholarship?" I asked. "That's a lot of money to give up."

"I thought you earned an academic one too," she said. "Is that not enough to cover your expenses?"

"It's enough to cover my classes and books, yes, but not the dorm or food plan," I said. "Although, in all honesty, I think I'd rather just live at home and commute; I wouldn't be in need of the soccer scholarship if I did that."

"Well, if it were me, I'd just rip off the Band-Aid and be done with it," she said, finishing her coffee.

"That's a lot easier said than done, Grandma," I said.

"Well, I guess I've always been one to face things head-on." She set her cup in the dishwasher and then walked over to me. "I've neither the time nor the inclination to pussyfoot around difficult situations. I say what I mean, and I mean what I say, and I will never back down from a fight." She placed her hand lovingly on my cheek. "Those same traits have been passed down to you, Adelaide; you just have to decide whether or not you're going to channel them."

"Thanks, Grandma," I smiled.

"You're welcome, dear." She then turned and headed toward the back door. "The world is no place for cowards, darling, so just put on your big girl panties and suck it up."

Chapter Three

"Addie, honey, is everything all right?" asked Mom. "You've seemed a bit preoccupied lately. Is there anything you want to talk about?"

Realizing that I was in no way prepared to discuss the dismantling of my soccer career right now, I looked directly into her eyes and lied straight through my teeth. "No, Mom, I'm fine. I'm just hoping that everything goes smoothly tonight, that's all. I know how important this night is to Brian and Aunt Christine."

Mom pulled out a few wine glasses and opened a bottle of cabernet sitting on the counter. "Yes, well, anytime your grandmother is in attendance, I tend to hope for the best and prepare for the worst." She poured the wine into a wine glass and imbibed greedily. "And in this case, I'm preparing for Armageddon."

"Don't you think you're being just a tad dramatic?" I asked. "Grandma can be a bit over-the-top, yes, but I think she'll eventually come to empathize with Nancy wanting a part of the wedding planning. I mean, this is Brian's wedding too, so it's natural for her to want to be involved. Surely she understands that."

"Addie, this is the same woman who thinks that the Spanish Inquisition was simply tough love for heretics," countered Mom. "Empathy is not her strong suit."

"Mom, that's a terrible thing to say," I gasped.

"What?" she shrugged. "It's the truth."

"Oh, for the love of God, Joan, you're just going to have to deal with it," said Grandma Helen, walking through the back door, her phone to her ear. "So they put you to sleep for a few minutes; you'll eventually wake up." She plopped into the chair next to me and motioned for Mom to pour a glass of wine. "Stop making this into something it's not. It's a colonoscopy, not open-heart surgery; you're not going to die."

Mom handed her a glass of wine, and she silently nodded her thanks.

"Listen, dear, I'm sitting here with Olivia and Addie, so I really must get off the phone. Just drink the solution the doctor gave you and eat your Jell-O. Tomorrow you'll be able to have that cheeseburger you've been talking incessantly about, and all will be fine, you'll see." She then clicked a button and ended the call. "My God, you would think that woman's dying."

"What's going on?" asked Mom.

"Oh, Joan's going in for a colonoscopy tomorrow and is afraid she won't wake up from the anesthesia," she said. "She's practically having a mental breakdown over it."

"Is it just routine or is something more going on?" asked Mom.

"It's just a routine check-up," said Grandma Helen, dismissively. "She's had them before, and everything has worked out fine, but this is Joan we're talking about, and you know how dramatic she can be."

"People in glass houses really shouldn't throw stones, Mother," said Mom.

"I may be dramatic, dear, but at least I'm rational," she countered. "Joan hasn't stopped obsessing over this thing since she started the prep two days ago; we are most definitely not the same."

"Okay, if you say so," said Mom, sipping her wine.

"I mean, the woman's as hearty as they come," continued Grandma Helen. "Two days on a liquid diet will probably do her some good; Lord knows she could use it."

"You know, you're being awfully callous towards Joan," said Mom. "Don't you think you should be a little more sympathetic to your friend's anxiety? She's obviously scared."

"It's a colonoscopy, Olivia, not a complex medical procedure," she scoffed. "I would be absolutely thrilled if it were me; I love colonoscopies."

"No one loves colonoscopies, Mother," said Mom. "That's an absolutely ridiculous claim."

"Well, I do," she shrugged. "I always have, really."

"Please explain to me what you find so wonderful about having to spend two full days cleaning out your colon so that the doctor can shove a scope up your rectum," said Mom. "It's an intrusive and unenjoyable procedure, and you know it."

"Ew, please tell me that's not something I'm going to have to do," I said, curling my lip. "That sounds awful."

"Don't worry, you have another thirty years to make peace with it," answered Mom. "But yes, at some point in your life you will have to have one."

"It's really not that bad, dear," said Grandma Helen. "You simply cleanse out your body, take a little nap, and go on with your life. And since it's a completely covered procedure, it's almost like getting a gift from the insurance company; I honestly can't wait to have mine next year."

"Have you completely lost your mind?" asked Mom.

"Darling, have you any idea how much weight you can lose?" she said. "I lost five pounds last time and couldn't have been happier; it was practically a godsend."

Mom looked at her as if she had just grown a third eye in the middle of her forehead. "There is something inherently wrong with you; I hope you know that."

"Oh please, most people think the way I do, darling," she said dismissively. "They may not like to admit it, of course, but secretly they do."

"No, Mom, I'm pretty sure you're on your own for this one," she said.

"Well, that's a pity," she sighed. "Then again, I've never really been one to look a gift horse in the mouth." She took a sip of wine and then asked, "So, where are we supposed to be meeting these people?"

"Their names are Tim and Nancy, Mother, you know this," said Mom. "And we're supposed to be meeting them at Prime 21."

"Well, I suppose there are worse places; at least we know the food will be decent." She absently toyed with the stem of her glass, "I take it we have a reservation?"

"No, actually we don't," answered Mom. "We thought the eleven of us would just walk in and surprise them. It always makes the dining experience so much more enjoyable when you have to wait an hour or two for a table."

"Your scintillating wit is as charming as ever, darling," she smiled. "But considering the fact that you want me to behave this evening, you may want to think about scaling back the sarcasm a bit."

"I'm sorry, Mom, that was uncalled for," she said, letting out a deep breath. "It's just that I really want this evening to go smoothly, and I guess I'm a little on edge."

"Oh, everything is going to work out fine, Olivia," she said, sliding her wine glass forward for a refill. "You've always been a worrier, even when you were a little girl. It's rather unfortunate that neither you nor your sister inherited my free-spirited ways."

"Okay, I'm here," said Aunt Christine, walking through the back door. She took a seat next to Grandma Helen and glanced down at her watch. "I figure we have a good hour before we need to leave, so let's go ahead and get the wine flowing."

Mom poured the last of the cabernet into a glass and handed it to her. "Ready for tonight?"

"I will be as long as you tell me there's another bottle waiting to be opened," she said, nodding at the empty one in Mom's hand. She took a quick sip and then added, "God, I can't believe how nervous I am."

"Why ever would you be nervous, darling?" asked Grandma Helen. "Your entire family is going to be there."

"Which is exactly my point," she said drolly.

"For God's sake, Christine, the world is not coming to an end," she chastised. "It's simply dinner. What's the worst that can happen?"

"Oh, I don't know, maybe Brian's parents will start to realize that their normal, well-adjusted son is marrying into a family of lunatics?" She took a deep breath and then let it out. "Look, I know I'm being ridiculous. I guess I was just hoping to stave off our family's crazy until after the wedding."

"Oh, now, where's the fun in that, dear?" winked Grandma Helen. "Crazy can be fun!"

"Please don't joke at a time like this, Mother," she moaned. "My nerves are frayed enough."

"You know, you really need to relax, darling," she sighed. "We've all promised to be on our best behavior tonight, and you have absolutely nothing to worry about."

Aunt Christine downed the last of her wine and then held it out to Mom. "In other words, pour me another."

***

An hour later we were walking into the lobby of Prime 21, an exclusive steakhouse that is located in the heart of downtown Canton. The interior has all of the charm of a high-end New York steakhouse with large, round tables draped in crisp white tablecloths, rich, dark mahogany paneled walls, plush red leather booths, and soft ambient lighting emanating from ornate crystal chandeliers and decorative sconces. The menu, with its top-tier, dry-aged, and wagyu beef offerings as well its seasonal farm-to-table accompaniments, makes this one of the best steakhouses in Georgia. I have only been here once, and I remember that the food was outstanding, and despite what Grandma Helen said earlier about there being worse places to dine, we all know that this is one of her favorite local restaurants.

"Do I seriously have to be here?" asked Beau. "I'm lending my support by being in the wedding. Isn't that enough?"

"Beau, this is an important night for your aunt, so please stop all the complaining," said Mom, sidling up next to him. "Besides, we're family, and this is what family does."

"So because I share a bloodline with you people, I'm now expected to attend all events leading up to this shindig?" he asked.

"Pretty much, yes," she nodded.

"Well, at least the bachelor party should be fun," he said.

"That one's off limits," said Mom. "And before you start arguing with me, the answer's no, you're only thirteen."

"Ugh, this bites," he snarled.

Ezra looked down at him and crossed his arms. "Dude, if Mom actually told you that you could go home, what would you do, exactly? It's not like you have any way of getting home, so the question is not only dumb but also moot."

"Which makes you an idiot," I chimed in.

"I'd take an Uber, Ezra, duh," he snapped. "So who's the idiot now, Addie?"

"Well, considering the fact that you haven't a penny to your name and absolutely no way to pay for one, I'd say that idiot would be you," said Dad, walking up behind him. He then turned toward the hostess and smiled. "Hi, we have a reservation at 7:00 under Jenkins, I believe."

The hostess looked down at the reservations list and said, "Oh, yes, you're the party of eleven. Three people have already arrived, so if you'll follow me, I'll take you to them."

"Oh, God, I'm going to be sick," said Aunt Christine. "I don't think I'm ready to do this."

"Listen, we're going to have to meet them eventually, Chrissy," said Mom. "So it's best if we just get this over with now and be done with it."

"Yes, but what if Mom makes a scene?" she asked. "Brian's parents actually like me right now, and I don't want any of that to change after they meet her."

"Mom knows how important this night is to you and Brian, and she has assured me that she will be on her best behavior," said Mom. "And, if she happens to step out of line, it just so happens I brought along a shock collar to subdue her."

Aunt Christine started giggling. "You always make me laugh, Ollie. Thank you."

As we followed the hostess toward the back of the restaurant, we could see that Brian and his parents were already seated at a large rectangular table having a discussion with the waiter.

"Now be sure to let them know that I want that martini as filthy as possible," said Nancy. "I like it ice cold and murky." She unfolded her napkin and placed it on her lap. "Oh, and don't forget, there needs to be three bleu cheese stuffed olives in the glass; not two, not four, but three."

"Yes, ma'am," nodded the waiter obediently. "Three olives, I understand."

"Not just olives," she said. "Bleu cheese stuffed olives."

"Of course, ma'am," smiled the waiter.

"Oh my God," said Mom, suddenly clutching my arm. "There's two of them."

Chapter Four

The moment we approached the table, Aunt Christine immediately walked over and hugged Tim and Nancy.

"It's wonderful to see you; thank you so much for coming!" she exclaimed. "I'm so excited to finally introduce you to my family."

"My God, can you believe the audacity of that woman?" hissed Grandma Helen, leaning in close to Mom. "I mean, how rude can you possibly be? Just let the poor boy do his job; he's not chattel for God's sake!"

"You're kidding, right?" asked Mom, lifting her brow. "She sounds exactly like you do on any given night."

"You take that back right now, Olivia Diane," she snarled. "I most certainly do not."

"And this is my sister Olivia and my mother, Helen," Aunt Christine smiled. "I'm sure you'll be seeing quite a lot of them over the next few months as we start planning the wedding."

As if on cue, Grandma Helen immediately whipped her head around and smiled radiantly as she walked over to embrace them.

"Well, hello there, my darlings," she trilled cheerfully. "Christine and Brian have told me so much about you. It's wonderful to finally be able to meet you in person."

"Yes, we've heard quite a bit about you too," said Nancy, awkwardly returning the embrace.

Taking a step back, Grandma Helen immediately gasped and dramatically placed her hand over her chest. "Oh, Nancy, you simply must tell me where you got that beautiful lavender scarf. It adds such a nice pop of color to your yellow pantsuit and really brings out the blue in your eyes. The entire ensemble is truly stunning!"

"Oh, well, thank you," said Nancy, slightly taken aback. "It was a gift, actually."

"Well, it's lovely, all the same," smiled Grandma Helen.

She then made her way over to the other side of the table and took a seat next to me. "Oh, dear God, that outfit is simply atrocious," she whispered. "Don't you ever allow me to go out in public looking like that."

"Hello, it's so nice to finally meet you," said Mom, extending her hand in greeting. "I hope you haven't been waiting too long."

"Not at all," answered Tim. "We actually only arrived a few minutes ago."

"You know, if you'd like, I'd be happy to track down our waiter so that you can order your drinks," said Brian. "I think he's just around the corner."

"Oh no, dear, that won't be necessary," said Grandma Helen, giving Nancy the side-eye. "I think the poor boy has quite enough on his plate as it is."

"Be nice, Mother," mumbled Mom quietly. "I don't want to have to kill you later."

"So, Anthony," Tim smiled. Brian tells me that you really know your way around a kitchen, and that you even owned an Italian restaurant at one point."

"It wasn't just an Italian restaurant, dear," interjected Grandma Helen proudly. "It was one of the best Italian restaurants in all of Georgia, and there were actually three of them."

"Yes, well, it did start out with one, dear," smiled Grandpa Anthony. "But yes, we eventually decided to open a few more in and around the North Georgia area. I've really only been retired for a few years, but I still love dabbling in the kitchen any chance I get."

"And you can make your own sausage to boot, from what I hear," said Tim. "That's really interesting. I'd love to watch you make it sometime."

"Well, I'd be more than happy to show you," replied Grandpa Anthony. "Why don't we look into scheduling something within the next few weeks?"

"I'd really like that," said Tim.

Just then the waiter came back and carefully set Nancy's martini in front of her. "How does that look, ma'am?" he asked.

"Honestly, it could use a little more olive juice, so if you would just bring some on the side, I'll do it myself." She lifted up the glass and pointed at it. "As you can see, it's clearly not dirty enough."

"It practically looks like swamp water, lady," mumbled Beau. "How much more dirt does it need?"

Mom turned and gently nudged him in his side. "Please keep your comments to yourself, Beau."

"Yes, of course," smiled the waiter. "I'll be right back with that."

"My God, the woman's an absolute tyrant," sneered Grandma Helen. "Has she no shame?"

"Let it go," said Mom quietly. "And for the record, I've watched you do the very same thing a time or two, so you may want to think about getting off that high horse of yours."

"Yes, but at least I do it with a smile on my face," she replied haughtily. "And not like I just sucked the juice out of an entire lemon."

"So Tim, I hear you used to be in finance," said Dad, continuing the conversation. "I'm sure that must have kept you busy."

"Oh, he wasn't just in finance, Greg," said Nancy. She turned her gaze toward Grandma Helen and smirked. "He was actually Senior VP for Goldman Sachs."

"Did you see that, Olivia?" hissed Grandma Helen. "That little remark was directed straight at me. You know, she's lucky I don't wipe that smirk right off her face."

"Yes, it did keep me very busy, but that was a long time ago," laughed Tim. "I'm old and quite happy to be retired now, although I do miss the craziness of it all from time to time." He took a quick sip of his scotch and then said, "So tell me, what is it that you do, Greg?"

As Dad launched into his spiel about his company and his role as key account manager, the waiter came by with a few baskets of freshly baked bread as well as Nancy's extra olive juice. Beau, never one to pass up on what he considers to be free food, immediately grabbed the breadbasket and withdrew two large pieces of sourdough that were barely able to fit on his bread plate.

"How about we save some for everyone else?" said Mom, taking the basket out of his hands and placing it back on the table. "You really don't need to be filling up on bread anyway."

"You can't expect someone to place a large basket of warm bread directly in front of me and then tell me not to fill up on it," he said. "It's super confusing and plays with my emotions." He picked up a silver ramekin sitting inside the breadbasket. "And look, even the butter is super soft; you can't possibly be that heartless."

"I'm not heartless, just practical," smiled Mom. "Besides, I'm fairly certain the two large pieces currently stacked on your plate will be more than enough to tide you over until your meal comes."

"So basically, your plan is to starve me," he said.

"Limiting your bread consumption is not starving you, Beau," she sighed. "Stop being so dramatic." She then turned her attention over to Grandma Helen. "So, what would you like to drink, Mom?"

"Certainly not that swill Nancy calls a martini, that's for sure," she said, curling her lip. "The woman may as well pop off the lid of an olive jar and just start gulping."

"Yeah, she was a bit over the top with that order," agreed Mom.

"A bit?" she repeated. "Darling, the woman could give Vladimir Lenin a run for his money; she's absolutely horrid."

"And what would you like to drink, ma'am?" asked the waiter as he stepped beside her.

"Oh, hello, dear, I didn't see you standing there," she cooed warmly. She picked up the wine menu and quickly read over it. "You know, you've already been so hard at work, I think I'll just make it easy on you and have a glass of the Willamette Valley Pinot Noir." She then handed the menu over to Mom. "And by the way, I want you to know that we used to own a few Italian restaurants, so I can completely empathize with how difficult some customers can be. Please know that you won't be having any of that from this side of the table."

Beau choked on his water and coughed out, "She's kidding, right?"

Mom simply smiled up at the waiter and said, "I'll have the Pinot as well, thank you." She then leaned in close to Grandma Helen and whispered, "Stop with antagonistic commentary, Mother; it's not only rude but obnoxious."

Once the waiter had finished taking everyone's drink orders, Nancy cleared her throat and addressed Mom. "So, Olivia, Christine tells me that you're a homeschooler. That must be a challenging endeavor, yes?"

"Well, it definitely helps keep the wine industry in business, that's for sure," laughed Mom. Noticing Nancy was not laughing along with her, she quickly added, "But yes, it is both challenging and rewarding; we're very blessed to be able to do it."

"I could never have homeschooled Brian," she sniggered. "The mere thought of being holed up in a house having to teach him what he's perfectly capable of learning in school is not something that's ever appealed to me." She took a sip of her martini. "It all just seems so backward and reminds me of *Little House on the Prairie.*"

Mom gave a weak smile and nodded her head in understanding.

"Yes, well, I can certainly see why you might think that way," she laughed. "The idea of schooling one's children can seem a bit foreign, but the one thing I've learned throughout the years is that there is no one in this world who knows my children better than me. No one else who understands their strengths and weaknesses, or knows when to push them, or when to scale it back. And quite honestly, there is no teacher, as wonderful as some may be, that will act as a greater champion for their success than me. It was definitely a huge sacrifice for our family when we chose to homeschool, but watching my children thrive and seeing firsthand how much they've learned over the years has made it all worth it."

"My daughter is one of the smartest people I know," interjected Grandma Helen. "And watching my grandchildren flourish under her tutelage and watching them far surpass all of their peers in both education and comportment has been an eye-opening experience. I personally never thought it was going to work, but thankfully I was proven wrong. Olivia has done a phenomenal job with both raising and educating them, and I couldn't be more proud of the job she's done."

"Wow, Mom, thank you," said Mom in surprise. "I never knew you felt that way."

"Yes, well, my grandchildren are brilliant human beings, and people need to know why," she replied. "You are my child, after all, so it only makes sense that you would excel in anything you do, including the education of your children."

"Ollie really has done a wonderful job with teaching them," said Aunt Christine. "Ezra is in his last year of avionics technician training, Addie is about to start her freshman year in college with both academic and soccer scholarships, and Beau is getting ready to begin his freshman year in high school where he will continue to learn Latin and logic along with all of his other subjects. It's really quite impressive."

"Well then, I suppose congratulations are in order," said Nancy, raising her glass. "That is most definitely a testament to your ability as both teacher and mother."

"Thank you," smiled Mom. "I really appreciate you saying that."

The waiter returned with our drinks and immediately began taking our dinner order. I could see that he was hesitant to approach Nancy and for good reason. The woman could give Meg Ryan in *When Harry Met Sally* a run for her money. The poor waiter had to practically use an entire page out of his server's pad in order to write down all of her specifications, which, in turn, prompted Grandma Helen to not only suppress her own demanding demeanor but also order like a normal person for once.

As soon as the waiter stepped away, Grandma Helen turned her attention to Nancy. "So tell me, Nancy, what is it that you like to do in your spare time?"

"Oh, a little bit of this and a little bit of that," she shrugged. "It really depends on my mood, I suppose."

"Do you enjoy going to the theater?" asked Grandma Helen.

"Oh, God no!" she exclaimed. "I can't stand watching any kind of theatrical performance or musical, it all just seems so trite and insignificant." She pulled a piece of bread from the basket and slathered it in butter. "No offense, of course. Christine has told us all about your budding theatrical career, but it's never been anything that has remotely interested me."

While our entire family braced for impact, the look on Grandma Helen's face remained surprisingly placid.

"Well, I suppose we all can't be cultured, now can we?" she mused. "The theater does tend to call to a more worldly and sophisticated individual."

Nancy peered amusingly over the rim of her martini glass. "Oh, I don't know about that, Helen. I suppose I just prefer challenging myself with reading the literary works of Dostoevsky, Tolstoy, and Hemingway rather than frittering away time with the simplistic renderings of something juvenile like *The Sound of Music.*" She took a sip and then added, "Oh, now wait a minute, that's supposed to be your next production, isn't it?"

Grandma Helen's jaw clenched as she looked over at the pleading eyes of Aunt Christine. She then calmly took in a deep breath and raised her gaze to meet Nancy's.

"Yes well, while there is no doubt that the three authors you mentioned are incredibly challenging to read, I honestly find the way in which they approach their storytelling to be strikingly different. For example, Dostoevsky is much more of an emotional and philosophical writer, choosing to focus on existential crisis and faith, whereas Tolstoy tends to be a little more detailed in his writing and often grapples with many historical and moral dilemmas. And then, of course, you have Hemingway, who differs not only in nationality but also offers a much more terse and minimal outlook in that he chooses to focus on personal struggles and stoicism rather than the indulgences that are so often associated with epicureanism."

She took a moment to sip her wine and revel in the shocked faces of everyone staring back at her. "But what it really comes down to, at least for me, Nancy, is experiencing the joy in life that comes with the act of performance. Yes, I suppose *The Sound of Music,* to some, may seem simplistic and unsophisticated, but it's also a very heartwarming story that embraces its audience and allows them to escape the everyday drudgery of the real world, even if only for a little while. So, while you prefer spending your time reading literary texts that solely focus on themes of suffering and despair, I prefer spending my time embracing the boundless creative, cultural, and historical exposure derived consistently from theatrical art."

The entire table remained completely silent as each one of us slowly digested the fact that Grandma Helen had not only succinctly summarized the writings of three of the greatest writers in both Russian and American literature but was also able to lend insight into the themes that permeated their work.

"Uh, I'm sorry, but can someone please tell me what exactly just happened?" asked Beau.

Chapter Five

"Well, that was fun," said Mom, placing her purse on the kitchen counter. "Nothing like a good verbal sparring match to bring family together." She crossed her arms over her chest and peered down at Grandma Helen. "Honestly, Mother, would it have killed you to be a little less smug?"

"I simply gave as good as I got, dear," she shrugged nonchalantly.

"Yes, but we specifically discussed being more amiable and benevolent when it comes to Tim and Nancy, or don't you remember?" asked Mom.

"If you're talking about the one-sided conversation we had in the car, and me agreeing to everything in order to get you to shut up, then yes, I do remember," she sighed. "Besides, that woman and her self-important attitude needed to be knocked down a few notches, and it just so happens that I was more than happy to do it." She crossed her arms to mimic Mom's stance. "And where exactly was Nancy's amiability and benevolence when she started to thumb her nose at both me and the theater? You know, you're always so quick to blame me, Olivia, but you and I both know she was the one to bare her claws first."

"Personally, I found it all to be quite entertaining," said Ezra, grabbing a bag of chips out of Beau's hands. "It kind of reminded me of Godzilla vs. Mothra, but with a lot less screeching."

"Hey, I was eating those!" exclaimed Beau.

"How is it that the two of you are even hungry right now?" asked Mom, turning to face them. "We literally just came back from dinner."

"All I know is that if I don't have to attend another family gathering until the day of the wedding, it will be entirely too soon," said Dad, opening the back door to let Churchill out.

Mom returned her attention to Grandma Helen. "And since when do you know anything about Russian and American literature? You hate reading anything that makes you have to you think."

"Oh, that," she giggled. "Christine happened to mention that Nancy liked those specific authors so, I simply Googled the three of them and committed the AI overview to memory."

"So, what, you're telling me you have an eidetic memory now, too?" asked Mom skeptically.

"I read scripts for a living, dear, it's really not that difficult," she smirked. "And honestly, I'm glad I did. I had a feeling that woman was going to try to belittle me in some way, so I just made sure to prepare myself to throw her obnoxiousness right back in her face." She picked a piece of lint off her lapel and looked back up at Mom. "And I must say that it worked too. The shocked expression on everyone's face, especially hers, was priceless."

"I'm so glad we could amuse you," drawled Mom.

"What does eidetic mean?" asked Beau.

"An eidetic memory is when a person can remember things in exact detail," answered Ezra. "It's kind of like a photographic memory."

"Man, that would be so cool!" he exclaimed excitedly. "It's almost like having a real-life superpower, you know?"

"Has anyone ever taken the time to watch this dog go to the bathroom?" interrupted Dad, completely changing the subject. He was standing by the door, watching Churchill navigate the backyard through the open blinds. "I mean, it's almost like he has some sort of methodology or something; it's fascinating, really."

"Ew, Dad, no!" I sneered. "That is so disgusting."

"I'm serious," said Dad. "He deliberately stops along certain points of a circle as if he has OCD or something."

"Oh yeah, he likes to do that," nodded Beau. "Let me guess, he's going in a counterclockwise rotation."

"Yeah, he is," said Dad. "How did you know?"

"I figured as much," said Beau. "He usually prefers going to the left. I like to call it Around the World in Five Minutes since that's how long it usually takes him to complete the whole circle."

"Dude, you actually have a name for it?" asked Ezra incredulously. "You're so weird."

"Shut up, Ezra," he snarled, grabbing the bag of chips back from him and walking over toward Dad. "Of course, every now and again he likes to switch it up and does some sort of zigzag pattern, but either way, he tends to be very particular about the way he chooses to relieve himself."

"Oh, yes, that reminds me," said Mom, snapping her fingers. "I need to make sure I order him more of the larger wipes." She pulled out a notepad and began shaking her head. "Last time, I mistakenly ordered the smaller ones, and he was not happy with me. I don't think they made him feel very clean."

"Oh, dear God, he's a dog, Olivia," said Grandma Helen. "How many times must I remind you of this?"

"Believe me, Helen, I've tried," said Dad. "It's taken me 28 years, but I've finally come to the realization that there is a definite hierarchy in this household, and neither the children nor I hold top billing." He plucked a wipe from the wipe warmer and opened the back door. "No, that title goes to the only one in this house who gets a treat after going potty."

"Here you go, my sweet baby," cooed Mom, getting down on her knees. She gently handed him a bacon-flavored treat. "Mommy is so proud of you."

"See what I mean?" he rolled his eyes.

"I honestly don't see what the problem is," said Mom, kissing Churchill softly on the head. "He's a good boy for going potty outside and needs to be acknowledged as such. "She took Dad's hand as he offered to help her back up. "In fact, I was even thinking about asking Chrissy and Brian if they would like Churchill to play a small part in the wedding. You know, maybe have him wear a special little tuxedo with the ring box around his neck. Wouldn't that be adorable?"

"Absolutely not!" exclaimed Grandma Helen. She pointed her finger down at Churchill. "That thing is not going to be in my daughter's wedding. Have you completely lost your mind?"

"I take it the last thirty seconds weren't enough to answer that question for you," mumbled Beau, reaching into the chip bag.

"Well, you don't have to be so rude about it," snapped Mom. "And Churchill is not a thing, he is an important member of this family, and I think Christine and Brian would love to include him in the wedding."

"Not if I have anything to say about it," said Grandma Helen. She picked up her purse and sidestepped awkwardly around Churchill, who was currently blocking her way to the back door. "I suppose I'll go and check on your father now, although I must say I'm still irritated that he made plans to go golfing with Tim tomorrow. He knows full well I can't stand his wife and he did it anyway."

"I think it's good that Dad's making new friends," said Mom. "He needs to get out of the house more."

"Oh, I definitely agree with you, dear," she said, opening the door. "I would just prefer that it not be with the husband of a diabolical and conniving bitch, that's all."

She closed the door and began walking up the path to the small house she shared with Grandpa Anthony.

"Okay, well, I can see it's the pot calling the kettle black again," snarked Beau.

***

Later that night, Ezra and I came into the kitchen for something to drink while my mom irritably emptied the dishwasher.

"You know, you people load the dishwasher like a scurry of squirrels on crack," she grumbled, pulling a bunch of dinner plates and stacking them in the cupboard next to the sink. "And for the record, I'm really tired of being the only one who ever empties it. Between your brother rigging it so that it never looks like it's been opened and the two of you conveniently ignoring it, it's always incumbent upon me to take care of it."

"Look, I understand your frustration, Mom, I really do," soothed Ezra, placing his arm around her. "The thing is, none of us want to add any more undo stress on you by not putting everything away where you want it. So, rather than upset the organization and systemization of your kitchen, we've simply decided to leave that solely to you." He then opened the refrigerator, grabbed a can of soda, and headed toward the back stairs. "Think of it more as a courtesy than anything else."

"A courtesy," she snarled, closing the dishwasher and walking over to the refrigerator. She pulled out a small white takeout container and placed it on the counter. "I suppose I can be just as courteous by taking a few bites of his leftover cheesecake." She pulled a fork from the utensil drawer and grinned wickedly. "We can't have him struggling to fit into his tux, now can we?"

"He's 6'8", Mom," I said. "Other than making sure his pants are long enough, he's never going to have that problem and you know that."

"Ugh, you're right," she grumbled, stuffing a large bite into her mouth. "I mean, who in their right mind even has the willpower to bring home cheesecake, anyway?"

As I sat there watching Mom devour over half of Ezra's cheesecake, I started to think about Grandma Helen's advice about ripping off the Band-Aid and coming clean about not wanting to play soccer anymore. Keeping it bottled inside was really beginning to take its toll, and rather than let it continue to fester, I figured it was probably best to just go ahead and get it over with.

"Hey Mom, can I talk to you about something?" I asked cautiously.

"Mm-hmm," she nodded, her mouth full of cheesecake.

I took a deep breath and slowly let it out. "Um, okay, well—"

"Hold on one second," she said, lifting her finger. "I need a glass of milk; this cheesecake is way too rich to be scarfed down in anger." She placed the takeout carton back into the refrigerator and pulled out the milk. "Ugh, now I feel sick."

She poured herself a small glass of milk and took a seat next to me. "Now, what is it that you wanted to talk about?"

As I opened my mouth to speak, tears immediately began to sting my eyes, and I started to cry uncontrollably.

"Honey, what's wrong?" she asked, immediately pulling me into her arms. "What's got you so upset?"

I tried to answer, but the tears kept getting in the way. I was so afraid of disappointing her that I couldn't speak. Soccer had been such an important part of not only my life but my parents' lives as well. There were so many years of driving me to and from practice, weekend games, and continual travel, that I didn't want them to resent me for wasting their time. My mother would literally school us all day, drive me to practice, and then wait in the car until I was finished. She never complained once. She had given so much of her time, and now I was going to look into her eyes and tell her that I was no longer interested in playing soccer and that I wanted to refuse the scholarship I had recently been offered.

"Addie, talk to me," she said softly. "I can't help you if you don't tell me what's wrong."

"I…I…" My tears were lodged deep in my throat. "I'm scared to tell you."

"Tell me what?" she asked, concern etched all over her face. "Honey, what's going on?"

"I don't want you to hate me," I sobbed.

"Sweetheart, I could never hate you," she said, squeezing me tighter. "I love you."

She stood there patiently letting me cry on her shoulder until I was finally able to breathe and get myself under control. As I slowly pulled away, I wiped my eyes, and whispered, "I don't want to play soccer anymore."

"You don't want to play soccer?" she asked, confused. "Has something happened?"

"No," I shook my head. "I'm just so tired of it taking all of my time. I'm tired of always having to train and be in the gym, and I know that college soccer is going to be even more demanding. I really just want to focus on school. I don't want all of my time to be filled with weekly games, travel, and gym workouts. I'm ready to lead a normal life, and if I'm being completely honest, I have for a long time. I was just too afraid to say it out loud."

"Oh, honey, I hate that you were too afraid to come to me with this," she said. "That is such a heavy burden to have to carry on your own, I wish you'd told me sooner so that I could have helped you through it."

"I didn't want you or Dad to be mad at me," I said, tears welling in my eyes again. "You have both sacrificed so much to allow me to play at a high level and I didn't want to let you down. I don't want you to feel that all of the money you spent on me has been wasted."

"Listen, your father and I love you with all of our hearts and we want you to be happy." She softly wiped away my tears. "And if that means you don't play soccer, then you don't play soccer. What matters to us more than anything is that you enjoy your life. Soccer isn't who you are, it never has been; it's just something you happen to do. Besides, I could see that you weren't loving it as much as you used to, but since you never said anything, I just figured it was the stress of having to figure out which college you wanted to attend."

"So you're really not mad at me?"

"Of course not," she smiled.

"You know that means that I'm going to have to continue living here," I said, reaching for a napkin. "My academic scholarships aren't enough to cover dorm and food expenses. Are you and Dad going to be okay with that?"

"Honey, you are aware that you're the main reason I stay sane around here, right?" she laughed. "Between the craziness of your grandmother, the snarkiness of your brothers, and everything else in between, I need all the help I can get." She kissed my forehead and pulled me in for another hug. "I'm just glad you didn't tell me you were pregnant because that would have definitely thrown me into a tailspin."

"Oh my God, Mom, are you serious?" I gasped, pulling away from her. "That's literally where your mind went?"

"Listen, your father and I are not ready to be grandparents, and I know without a shadow of a doubt that your grandmother would raise holy hell if she found out that she was going to be a great-grandmother, so when you started crying hysterically, it was the only thing that came to mind."

"Mom, you know me better than that," I admonished. "I would never be that stupid."

"I know that, baby," she sighed. "But when you're a parent of adult children, you tend to worry about things like that."

"Oh, my God, can you imagine what Grandma would say?" I asked.

"She'd probably curl up in a corner with a box of wine and a bottle of Valium until she was able to convince herself that she's living in an alternate universe," quipped Mom. "Well, either that or she'd kill you."

We both started laughing uncontrollably at the thought of Grandma Helen's mental breakdown at the news of having to become a great grandmother when Aunt Christine barged in through the back door.

"Alright, what exactly was all that back at the restaurant?" she spat. "And when in the hell did our mother become a frigging Mensa member.

CHAPTER SIX

The next morning, Mom, Aunt Christine, and I were in the kitchen going over the day's itinerary when Grandma Helen walked in through the back door. She hastily made her way over to the coffee pot and let out a sigh of relief when she saw that it was half full.

"Oh, thank God, there's still some left." She opened the refrigerator and pulled out the creamer. "I was worried I'd be too late."

"You know, last time I checked, you have a perfectly good Keurig sitting on your kitchen counter that is specifically made to brew coffee," said Mom.

"Yes, dear, I know," she said, filling her cup. "I'm the one who bought it, remember?"

"Then why aren't you using it?" asked Mom.

"Well, if you must know, I've learned that I really don't have the patience to sit and wait for it to brew." She placed the creamer back into the refrigerator. "It just takes too much time and effort."

"It's a single serve coffee maker, Mother, it takes less than 30 seconds," answered Mom.

"Yes, but then your father makes me throw away the little cup thingy, clean up all the loose coffee grounds, and fill the water back up." She stirred her coffee and took a sip. "It's just easier to come here and have it done for me."

"You do realize that is the epitome of laziness, yes?" said Aunt Christine.

"Lazy is such an ugly word, dear," she sniffed haughtily. "I much prefer the term selective participation; it just has a better ring to it. A certain 'je ne sais quoi,' if you will."

"Oh, so we're now adding French to our vast repertoire of knowledge, are we?" drawled Aunt Christine, sarcastically. "What's next, Mother, a master's thesis on the cognitive, neural, and behavioral traits of the Kasakela chimpanzee community of Tanzania? You know, if you play your cards right, you and all of your AI summaries may just be able to give Jane Goodall a run for her money."

"Ugh, must we do this now?" sneered Grandma Helen, rolling her eyes. "I haven't consumed anywhere near enough caffeine to endure a long lecture from you, Christine."

"Well, you may want to go ahead and start guzzling, then, because I have a lot to say," she retorted sourly.

"Honestly, dear, I don't know why you're so upset," shrugged Grandma Helen. "We ended the evening civilly, didn't we?"

"That's not the point, Mother, and you know it," she said, irritably.

The look of confusion on Grandma Helen's face led Mom to intervene.

"I think what Chrissy's trying to say is that going on the attack after arming yourself with enough literary knowledge to win a category of *Jeopardy*, may not have been the best way to handle the situation, that's all."

"That's all?" repeated Grandma Helen, arching her brow. "You can't possibly be serious."

"Listen, Mom—," started Aunt Christine.

"No, you listen!" she spat. "That woman was not only rude and arrogant, but she belittled the one thing in my life that I love to do. She was callous, cruel, and completely out of line, and I'm sorry, but there is no way in hell that I will ever stand down and keep quiet while someone condescendingly attacks me and the things I care about." She held up a finger and pointed accusingly at Mom and Aunt Christine. "And the two of you, more than anyone, should know this because I've taught you both to do the same."

As we sat there silently, registering what she had just said, a soft, continual ding echoed in the distance.

"I understand what you're saying, Mom, I really do," said Aunt Christine penitently. "And I'm so sorry that Nancy made you feel that way. She had absolutely no right to belittle you like that, and I hate that you were hurt because of it." She took Grandma Helen's hand in her own and breathed in deeply. "And I know that it's a lot to ask, but I'd really appreciate it if you'd be willing to suppress your irritation with Nancy.

We're all going to be spending a lot of time together over the next few weeks, and one of you is going to have to step up and keep the peace."

"Ugh, keeping the peace is not really my forte, dear, you know that," she groaned. "But if it means that much to you, then I suppose I can give it a try."

Ding.

"Thank you, Mom," she smiled. "I can't tell you how much that means to me."

Ding.

"And just so you know," said Grandma Helen. "I'll be expecting a case of wine for my compliance. My verbal and emotional restraint is going to need it after multiple weeks of this."

"Yes, of course," nodded Aunt Christine. "I wouldn't dare think otherwise."

"And nothing cheap, either," she added. "You know how much I despise anything that costs less than $40."

Ding.

"I'm well aware, Mother," she grumbled.

"Okay, well, now that that's settled, I suppose I'm going to need a bit of wine in order to mentally prepare myself for the day." She reached for a bottle of cabernet sitting on the counter. "Not killing Nancy is going to take a lot of effort on my part, and I find that I'm much more amenable after a glass or two."

"You're not going to have to worry about any of that today, Mother," said Aunt Christine. "Nancy apparently chipped a tooth on something last night and now has to go to the dentist to get it repaired. She's apparently in quite a bit of pain."

"Oh, thank God," sighed Grandma Helen, with relief. "Perhaps even more calamities will fall upon her, and we won't have to worry about her at all."

"That's not being the bigger person, Mother," cautioned Mom.

Ding.

"Oh, relax, Olivia, I'm only kidding." She took a quick sip of coffee and began glancing around the room irritably. "And for God's sake, what is that incessant dinging sound?"

"Um, I'm pretty sure it's coming from my phone," answered Mom. "I think it may be my text messages."

"Who in the world would be texting you that much?" asked Aunt Christine.

"Uh, that would be my husband," she said, smiling thinly.

Ding.

"Well, you may want to answer him, then," she said. "It might be something important."

"Trust me, it's not," replied Mom, drolly. "He does this every morning whenever he's sitting on the toilet. It's becoming a common occurrence."

"Ugh, that's an image I could have done without this morning," said Grandma Helen, curling her lip. "Maybe I'm going to need that wine after all."

"I'm sorry, he does what?" asked Aunt Christine in confusion.

"Anytime Dad spends time in the bathroom, he likes to share Instagram posts," I explained. "He actually shares them with all of us. If my phone were down here, you'd be hearing it go off too."

Ding.

"And you say he does this every morning?" asked Grandma Helen. "Whatever for?"

"I think it helps him pass the time," I said.

"Yes, I understand that, dear, but why send them to all of you?" she pressed.

"He likes sharing things that he thinks might interest us," answered Mom. "I think it's sweet."

"Well, I think it's annoying," sneered Grandma Helen.

"If you find that it gets to be too much for you, you're certainly free to take your coffee on the go, Mother," smiled Mom. "Better yet, you can even start brewing and drinking your own coffee in your own kitchen and not have to worry about it at all."

"And deprive you of the joy of having me here every morning?" she retorted sarcastically. "Never!"

"Mom, will you please tell Dad to stop sending me Instagram posts every time he sits on the toilet?" snarled Beau, coming down the back stairs. "It's like having to deal with a chihuahua on crack every time he hits the share button."

"Your father is simply sharing videos he thinks you may be interested in, Beau," said Mom. "There's no need to be nasty about it." She rinsed her cup out in the sink. "In fact, you may find that you actually learn something from some of those videos."

"Learning is overrated," he deadpanned.

"Why don't you just turn off your notifications, dear?" smiled Grandma Helen. "That's what I do whenever your mother texts me."

"Are you serious, Mom?" she exclaimed. "What if there's an emergency and I need to get hold of you?"

"I'm sure I'd get one of your hundreds of messages at some point, dear," she said dismissively. "You tend to be very tenacious whenever you need something."

"Do you do this to Dad too?" asked Aunt Christine.

"Oh, God no," she snickered. "He never keeps me on the phone as long as you and your sister do; he knows better than that."

"Wait, so you do that to me, too?" she gasped. "What the hell, Mom?"

"Well, what do you expect, Christine?" she countered. "I have a life to live, and I can't always be talking on the phone with the two of you." She looked up at the clock. "Oh, that reminds me, I need to go and pick up my new script from the theater. What time are we leaving to go dress shopping, again?"

"10:30," answered Aunt Christine irritably.

"Excellent, I'll be back in plenty of time!" She walked out the back door and called out over her shoulder, "Don't call me, girls, I'll call you!"

"Can you believe the nerve of that woman?" asked Aunt Christine.

"Unfortunately, yes, I can," said Mom. "You know, there are many days when I find myself wishing we had a more sincere and nurturing mother, but alas, that is not to be."

"It's been 50 years, Mom, maybe it's time to give up the dream," said Beau, pouring himself a bowl of cereal.

"I'm only 46, Beau!" she shrieked.

"Are you really?" he said, casually. "Huh, I guess you really do learn something new every day."

"You're such an idiot," I snapped.

"Bite me," he retorted.

"Okay, before this has a chance to escalate any further," interjected Mom, "I suggest that we all take our leave and start getting ready for the day." She looked down at Beau while he ate his cereal. "And don't forget, Dad is expecting you to help him in the garage later, so please be sure to be here when he's ready to get started."

"Yes, ma'am," he sighed. "I'm well aware that I am nothing but a slave in this household."

"A slave that is both loved and well taken care of," she smiled, kissing him on the forehead. "Besides, it's not like you have anything else going on today."

"I would if I had money and/or transportation," he grumbled.

"You know, it just so happens that there are numerous chores to be done around here that will earn you plenty of money," she said. "I'd be happy to make you a list."

"Yeah, well, your definition of plenty is completely contradictory to mine, so I think I'll pass," he snarked.

"Suit yourself," she said with a shrug.

He watched her turn to leave and then called out nonchalantly. "Oh, and by the way, I think I might be going blind."

"I'm sorry, what?" she asked in confusion.

"I think I'm going blind," he reiterated, taking a bite of his cereal.

"Don't be ridiculous, Beau," she said dismissively. "And even if you were, you're still not getting out of helping your father in the garage."

"No, I'm totally serious," he insisted. "I'm seeing flashes of light whenever it's really dark outside. I've looked it up and I think I have retinal detachment."

"What have I told you about looking symptoms up on the internet?" said Mom, putting her hands on her hips. "Everything you read tells you that you're going to die, so please, just stop."

"It never mentioned dying!" he exclaimed. "Do you think I'm going to die?"

"No, I don't." She shook her head. "I was just making a point."

"Look, I already have floaters in my eyes, so this just seems like the natural progression, you know?" he responded. "I'm just trying to be prepared for the inevitable, that's all."

"Honey, we went to the optometrist about your eyes two months ago, and the doctor said it's perfectly normal to have floaters. You have absolutely nothing to worry about." She stepped toward him and softly brushed the hair away from his face. "Besides, if there had been any kind of retinal detachment, he would have seen it."

"Yeah, if he was looking for that, but he wasn't," he countered.

"Son, when he shines that light into your eyes, he can see everything behind it. Trust me, he would have seen it." She kissed him softly on the cheek. "I tell you what, why don't we give it a few days, and if it still continues to happen, we'll set up an appointment and go back to see Doctor Matthews."

"Okay, fine," he relented. "But if I end up not having enough time to prepare myself mentally for a life of sightlessness, then that's all on you."

Chapter Seven

"Oh dear God, who in their right mind would even think to wear something like this?" asked Grandma Helen, holding up a mid-length, mustard-colored dress covered in black lace and ruffles. "It's absolutely grotesque!"

"Would you please keep your voice down?" hissed Mom. "I'm really not in the mood to make apologies for your behavior today."

"Honestly, dear, the apology should be coming from whomever it was that agreed to allow this atrocity into the store," she retorted sourly. "Anyone with an ounce of taste can see that this thing has Walmart Rollback written all over it."

"Seriously, Mom, you need to stop," said Aunt Christine. "Someone might actually overhear you."

"Would you two stop being so dramatic?" scolded Grandma Helen, placing the dress back onto the rack. "I'm simply expressing my opinion, which, last time I checked, was still legal in this country." She slowly sauntered her way around the store. "Besides, I think you'll find that most people would agree with me." She paused momentarily. "Well, people with taste, that is."

"I'm curious," said Aunt Christine, leaning in close to Mom. "Do you think she's already forgotten why we're really here?"

"Forgotten, no," said Mom, shaking her head. "Conveniently postponing the reason in her ADHD-addled mind, yes."

We had barely stepped foot into Magnolia's Bridal Boutique when Grandma Helen immediately abandoned us to begin shopping for herself. Now, I know this may seem strange considering Magnolia's is primarily a bridal shop, but in addition to selling high-end wedding gowns, they also carry a wide array of elegant evening dresses from designers like Chanel,

Yves Saint Laurent, and Giorgio Armani (which, according to Grandma Helen, is the venerated trinity of designer clothing). So, when you combine all of that, along with her rare ability to think outside of herself, it makes perfect sense that the three of us would find ourselves sitting here, bored out of our minds, waiting for her to finish.

Of course, Grandma Helen's self-centeredness is nothing if not predictable, so it only makes sense that Mom and Aunt Christine would secretly start shopping last weekend for wedding dresses. You see, by preemptively narrowing down the dress selection, they were hoping to create an enjoyable shopping experience with little stress, zero drama, and no bloodshed, which, when shopping with Grandma Helen, is always a possibility.

"Oh, now this is absolutely gorgeous!" exclaimed Grandma Helen. She held up a floor-length, Yves Saint Laurent knit dress with a matching cinched-waisted jacket and made her way over to the closest mirror. "And it complements my skin tone perfectly, don't you think?" She spent another few minute's preening in front of the mirror before letting out an irritable sigh. "Are the three of you planning on helping me shop, or are you just going to sit there like bumps on a log?"

"I'm not really sure, Mother," answered Mom. "I suppose that depends on how much longer you plan on hijacking Christine's shopping day."

"I'm sorry; I wasn't aware that I was hijacking anything," said Grandma Helen, coolly. "I simply paused momentarily to look at a few dresses on our way to the bridal area, but maybe that's just a little too much to ask of you today."

"Momentarily?" said Aunt Christine. "Mom, it's been thirty minutes!"

"Ugh, fine," she relented, raising her hand to get the attention of the salesgirl standing nearby. "I suppose finding your dress does take priority."

"Gee, you think?" snarked Aunt Christine.

"I'll have you know that the mother-of-the-bride plays a very important role in all of this, Christine," she said emphatically. "People will be looking at me long before you even step foot down that aisle, so it's imperative that I look utterly fabulous." She held the dress back up for a final inspection. "People will be talking about me for days!"

"Oh, I'm sure they'll be talking about you, alright," said Mom, rolling her eyes.

"Is there something I can help you with?" asked the salesgirl. "I think I saw you motioning for me to come over."

Grandma Helen smiled magnanimously and handed the gold dress over to her, making it a point to read her name tag. "Darla do be a dear and take this over to the dressing room for me. Unfortunately, my attention is needed elsewhere, but rest assured, I have every intention of coming back to do more shopping."

"Yes, of course," said Darla. "I'll go and hang this up in room number five."

"Thank you, darling," she cooed. "Oh, and please make sure that we have plenty of champagne over in the bridal area. We're on the hunt for the perfect wedding gown and must keep ourselves properly hydrated!"

***

Twenty minutes later, Grandma Helen sullenly sipped her champagne while waiting for Aunt Christine to model the first dress.

"I just don't understand," she said, shaking her head despondently. "What kind of bride goes dress shopping only to try on two dresses?"

"The kind who knows exactly what she's looking for, so just back off, okay?" answered Mom.

"Yes, but even that obesely rotund woman in the next dressing room over has more dresses than her," she said, gesturing toward the changing area. "I don't know what surprises me more, the fact that Christine found so few or that she found so many."

"I would think that this would make you happy," said Mom. "The sooner we finish with Christine, the sooner we can get back to shopping for you, which, as we all know, is what you want anyway." She took a sip of champagne and wrinkled her brow in confusion. "And what difference does it make how many dresses that other woman is trying on? We're here for Christine, remember?"

"Because fat people have fewer choices, Olivia!" she hissed. "Christine is a quarter of that woman's size, so if she's able to find multiple dresses that she can stuff her fat body into, your sister should have at least triple that amount."

"This isn't a contest, Mother!" exclaimed Mom. "Besides, Christine's perfectly capable of figuring out how many wedding dresses she wants to try on."

"I understand that," answered Grandma Helen, irritably. "I'm just worried she's going to sell herself short again this time, that's all."

"What do you mean, 'sell herself short?'" asked Mom.

She took a deep breath and slowly let it out. "Jack completely ruined her first wedding with all of his ridiculous demands, and I'm just concerned that she's going to take a backseat to all of the planning like she did back then. I want this wedding to be perfect for her; she deserves that after what she went through with him."

"And it will be, I promise," soothed Mom. "Brian is nothing like Jack. He encourages her in ways that Jack never would, and as far as the wedding planning goes, he's given her carte blanche to do whatever she wants. Believe me, she's got it completely under control."

"Yes, but why only two dresses?" she pouted. "It just doesn't make any sense."

"Mom, I think you need to tell her the truth about you and Aunt Christine going shopping last week," I said, whispering into her ear. "It'll help her to make sense as to why there are only two dresses."

"No, that's a terrible idea, absolutely not," she said, shaking her head.

"It's not like it's that big of a deal," I pressed. "I'm sure she'll understand."

"I'm sorry, but have you even met your grandmother?" she asked sarcastically. "Heads will roll, believe me."

"Whose head is going to roll, darling?" asked Grandma Helen, tuning herself into the conversation.

"Uh, the wedding planner," said Mom, her eyes growing wide, indicating that I should play along. "You know, if she tries to convince Chrissy and Brian not to have an open bar at the reception."

"What?" she exclaimed loudly. "Oh no, she won't! If that woman thinks for one minute that we're not having an—"

The rest of Grandma Helen's sentence immediately died in her throat as she watched the young woman in the dressing room next to Aunt Christine slowly waddle her way over to the pedestal platform that was standing in front of us.

"Oh dear God, she looks like a sequined enshrouded silo with legs," muttered Grandma Helen, seeming to get her voice back.

"Please control yourself, Mother," said Mom quietly. "We're all seeing what you're seeing, and don't need a play-by-play."

"You know, she kind of looks like Alyson Hannigan from *How I Met Your Mother*," I said.

"If Alyson Hannigan swallowed a fully inflated 32-inch round plastic beach ball, then yes, I guess I can see that," said Grandma Helen.

"You know, now that I think about it, maybe you should try on the next one," said the salesgirl, desperately trailing after her. "That way, I can see if we can order this one in a larger size for you."

The dress she was wearing was practically bursting at the seams and literally looked as if it were about to pop open on either side like a can of biscuits.

"Oh, but this one is so beautiful!" she gushed, struggling to make her way onto the platform. "You know, I've always wanted a mermaid-style wedding dress ever since I watched *The Little Mermaid*." She caught sight of the salesgirl standing behind her in the lighted mirror and smiled brightly. "This dress makes me feel just like Ariel!"

"Yes, but it makes you look like a muted version of Ursula, the sea witch," muttered Grandma Helen. "Except with better hair."

"Play nice, Mother," warned Mom.

"I am playing nice," she shrugged defensively. "I just said she had nice hair, didn't I?"

"You know, I think you may be right," said the young woman, feeling herself around the waist. "It does seem to be fitting a little bit tight. Maybe it would be best to go up one more size."

"Only one?" muttered Grandma Helen.

"Stop," said Mom, through gritted teeth.

"The woman looks like a fat piece of sausage bursting out of its casing, Olivia," she spat. "Unless it's tent-sized, it's not going to work; even you can see that."

"Yes, but must you always be so rude about it?" asked Mom.

"No, I don't have to be rude, I just choose to be," she answered flippantly. "I always find it gets my point across better."

As we watched the young bride-to-be trundle her way back into her dressing room, the door to Aunt Christine's room opened, and the three of us sat there completely stunned, mesmerized by how beautiful she looked. The gown she wore was absolutely breathtaking, exuding both elegance and sensuality with a sleek, minimalist silhouette, luxurious satin fabric, and a deep plunging V-neckline. The soft ivory gown hugged her body perfectly, flowing seamlessly to the floor; the lustrous, subtle train following directly behind. What I loved most, however, was the sleeveless design that allowed for two long cape-like panels on either side to drape regally over her shoulders, creating a soft, feminine, and ethereal effect that made it look both effortlessly chic and modernly sophisticated at the same time.

"Oh, Chrissy," exclaimed Mom. "It's simply stunning!"

"You look absolutely beautiful," I said, admiringly.

"You know, this only recently came into the store," said the salesgirl, fanning out the small train behind her as Aunt Christine stepped onto the platform. "In fact, you're the first person I've seen try it on. It looks absolutely amazing on you."

"Thank you so much, I really appreciate you saying that." She glanced at herself in the mirror and said, "I really think this is the one."

"It's perfect," said Mom. "It's absolutely perfect."

Aunt Christine looked back over her shoulder at Grandma Helen with concern etched on her face. "Do you like it, Mom?"

Grandma Helen, who rarely gets emotional, stood up and walked over to her with tears in her eyes, reverently taking her hand. "You are truly the epitome of grace and elegance, Christine, and this dress is the perfect extension of that."

"Thank you, Mom," she smiled.

Refusing to let go of her hand, she continued. "I truly hope you realize what an extraordinary woman you are, and how fortunate Brian is that you agreed to marry him." A tear rolled slowly down her cheek. "So yes, while this dress is absolutely exquisite, it's the woman wearing it that really makes it stand out, always remember that."

"Oh, Mom," sniffed Aunt Christine, wiping a tear from her eye. "You have no idea how much that means to me."

"You deserve to be happy, darling," she smiled. "And I genuinely pray that you've finally found your prince."

"I have, Mom," she said. "He's everything I've ever wanted and more."

"Good," she nodded, lovingly cupping her cheek. "Because if he's not, I'll gut him like a pig."

"Wait, what?" asked Aunt Christine, in confusion. "What did you just say?"

"I said I'll gut him like a pig, dear," she repeated, nonchalantly.

She then turned on her heel and headed back toward the designer gown section of the store, calling out jovially, "Oh, Darla, darling, I'm ready to go shopping now!"

Chapter Eight

The rest of the afternoon was spent watching Grandma Helen try on dress after dress while working poor Darla to death. I'm telling you that girl earned every penny of her commission, and then some. If it wasn't a different size, she was tracking down, it was a different color. If the color wasn't just right, then she needed to find something that was. She was also expected to keep Grandma Helen's champagne glass filled, which as we all know, is a feat in and of itself, so finally, after the fourth refill, Darla got smart and decided to leave two chilled bottles just outside of her dressing room.

Thankfully, a selection was eventually made, and Darla's time in purgatory could finally come to an end. The poor girl looked simply ragged, and as we made our way out the door, purchases in hand, I briefly glanced back to find her chugging the remainder of the champagne, straight from the bottle, as her coworker stared on in open-mouthed disbelief.

It's sad, really, but Grandma Helen tends to have that effect on people, especially those in any type of service industry. There is, however, one person who stands out among the rest. One who not only tolerates her drama, but equally matches it. And, as strange as it may sound, he knows exactly how to handle her theatrics better than anyone outside of our family.

His name is Justin Perdue, a flamboyantly middle-aged gay man who has been serving Grandma Helen the perfect dirty martini for over seven years now. Of course, this wasn't always the case. In the beginning, Justin did everything he could to avoid her. He would give her table away, pretend his section was full, or act as if he didn't see her. He even went so far as to hide in the walk-in freezer in order to stay away from her, but unfortunately, that only ended in catastrophe, as he was eventually admitted to the hospital with a terrible case of pneumonia and frostbite.

I guess it's true what they say about hitting rock bottom because ever since that horrible experience in the walk-in, Justin has been beyond receptive to Grandma Helen's presence. He's either started meditating, medicating, or has found religion because the man is practically a saint. He tolerates her imperious nature with ease, placates her melodramatic idiosyncrasies with grace, and genuinely seems happy to see her. Which, quite honestly, is a good thing because she's currently making a complete spectacle of herself, and us, vying for his attention across the entire restaurant.

"Justin!" Grandma Helen waved riotously. "Oh, Justin, darling, we're here!"

"You know, maybe we should just talk to the hostess about seating us in his section rather than alerting the entire restaurant that we're here," said Mom. "Not to mention the fact that Justin probably doesn't appreciate being beckoned across the room like a golden retriever."

"Oh, please, Olivia, the man adores me," scoffed Grandma Helen. "He loves it when I do things like this. It makes him feel special."

"Yes, but everyone is staring at us, Mother," said Aunt Christine. "Could you at least tone it down a little?"

"When have you ever known me to tone anything down, Christine?" she quipped. "Besides, I forgot to call him and tell him that we're coming. You know how much he likes to be prepared."

"Warned is more like it," snarked Mom.

"Helen, darling!" exclaimed Justin, bending down to hug her. "I thought you weren't coming in until tomorrow. You know how I like to have your martini at the ready whenever you come in."

"Yes, well, wedding dress shopping took quite a bit longer than we anticipated and has completely zapped us of all of our energy. So, we thought we'd pop in for a few martinis and an early dinner." She dramatically placed her hand over her chest, feigning concern. "Please tell me you have room for us."

"Of course, my darling, anything for you," he gushed. "Let me just grab a few menus first."

"You're an absolute godsend, darling," she trilled. "Thank you!"

"Yes, darling, I know," he winked.

"Alright, listen, Mother," hissed Aunt Christine, stepping up beside her. "I really don't appreciate you insinuating that it was me that took all afternoon to shop. I was the one who was done in under thirty minutes, remember? You're the one who ended up turning it into a three-hour, one-person runway spectacle!"

"My God, Christine, what's got you in such a tizzy?" she asked.

"I just hate it when you make things into something they're not, Mother, that's all," she said. "We were shopping, end of story."

"Well, to be fair, we were in a bridal shop looking for your wedding dress, so technically that would fall under the guise of wedding dress shopping, no?" clarified Grandma Helen.

"Yes, but—," she began.

"Don't, Chrissy," whispered Mom. "Just hop off the carousel of crazy now, before you get sucked in any further."

"Fine," said Aunt Christine, taking Mom's advice. "Let's just eat."

"And drink!" added Grandma Helen, merrily. "We certainly don't want to forget that."

"Okay, so you must tell me, were you able to find what you were looking for?" asked Justin, walking back over to us. "You know, the perfect dress that's going to stop everyone in their tracks and make them yearn to be you?"

Aunt Christine was just about to answer that question when Grandma Helen immediately cut in.

"Oh, darling, did I!" she raved. "And you are absolutely going to love it!"

We followed Justin to our table, listening to Grandma Helen regale him with a detailed description of her dress. "It's a stunning floor-length, champagne-colored, Oscar de la Renta, crystal-embroidered gown that looks as if it were made specifically for me. It is simply breathtaking and will definitely be turning heads!"

"Ooh, that sounds extraordinary!" he boomed, excitedly. "You know how I absolutely adore anything made from Oscar."

"Oh, you and I, both, darling," replied Grandma Helen. "I practically had to scour that whole place in order to find it, and when I did; I wept with joy, I was so happy!"

"Uh, don't you mean Darla had to scour the place?" drawled Mom. "I'm pretty sure you were just sitting there, drinking champagne the whole time."

"I think poor Darla was crying too, but not happy tears, that's for sure," added Aunt Christine, sourly.

"Well, technically, yes, it was Darla, but I'm the one who had to tell her where to go," retorted Grandma Helen, indignantly. "And Darla wasn't crying, Christine. She was incredibly helpful, and I told her as much right before we left."

"Oh, my darling, you must be absolutely parched," said Justin. "I tell you what, I'm going to get you a martini so that you can relax and take it easy for a while, and maybe build back your strength."

"Jesus, it's not like she ran the Boston Marathon, Justin," snarked Aunt Christine.

"You know, I think a filthy martini is exactly what I need, darling, thank you," said Grandma Helen, ignoring the slight. "It'll be the perfect little pick-me-up!"

"Shall I go ahead and make it three, then?" asked Justin, glancing around the table.

"Three would be wonderful, darling," smiled Grandma Helen. "Oh and be sure to bring my beautiful granddaughter anything she wants." She patted my hand softly. "She was such a trooper today."

"An iced tea would be great, thanks," I said.

As soon as Justin came back with our drinks, Grandma Helen jubilantly raised her martini glass. "To a very successful day of shopping!" she boasted.

"Salute!" we said, raising our glasses.

Grandma Helen continued to lift her glass. "I'd also like to make a very special toast to my beautiful daughter, Christine, who is going to look absolutely stunning walking down the aisle in that amazing dress. You were truly breathtaking, my darling."

"Thanks, Mom," smiled Aunt Christine. "I hope Brian thinks so too."

"The man will be in awe of you, my dear," she winked.

"He really is going to love it, Aunt Christine," I smiled. "He'll probably even tear up when he sees you—."

"Oh, my God, this is beyond perfect!" interrupted Grandma Helen, greedily sipping her martini. "I say we go ahead and order another round."

"I think I'm only going to have one tonight," said Mom. "I still have a few things I need to get done once I get home."

"Are you serious?" guffawed Aunt Christine. "You never say no to a good martini."

"I didn't say no," she said, holding up her glass. "I'm having one right now, aren't I?"

"Oh, darling, even I don't believe myself when I say I'm only going to have one drink," snickered Grandma Helen. "I'm not that delusional."

"I'm sure the boys are perfectly capable of taking care of themselves for one night," said Aunt Christine. "Besides, Greg's there; he can handle it."

As if on cue, Mom's phone began to ring, the caller ID showing that it was Ezra.

"Hi honey," she answered, putting it on speaker. "Is everything alright?"

"Not really, no," he replied somberly. "I think I might be going deaf."

"Oh dear God, not you, too," she sighed, closing her eyes despondently. "I honestly don't think I'm able to handle more than one hypochondriac episode at a time, Ezra."

"I'm not a hypochondriac, Mom!" he said irritably. "I'm just concerned that I'm not going to be able to hear anymore. And what do you mean, 'not you, too?' Is there someone else in the family going deaf?"

"Not exactly, no," answered Mom. "It's just that your brother seems to think that he's going blind."

"Wait, Beau's going blind?" asked Aunt Christine, confused.

"No," said Mom, rolling her eyes. "He just thinks he is."

"My God, what in the world is going on at your house?" asked Grandma Helen. "Should we alert child protective services?"

"Nothing is going on, Mother," she snapped. "And stop saying things like that; it's not funny!

"Oh, don't get so uppity, Olivia; you know I'm only joking," she scoffed. "We all know you're a wonderful mother, so just drink your martini and relax."

"Hold on a minute," interrupted Ezra, his voice rising. "You mean to tell me that I'm sitting here going deaf and you're out drinking martinis?"

"Well, to be fair, dear, we did order our drinks long before we found out you were losing your hearing," called out Grandma Helen. "So you can't really blame your mother for that because she didn't know."

"Thank you, Mother," drawled Mom.

"Of course, darling," she grinned. "Do you think he was able to hear me?"

"I'm pretty sure the whole restaurant heard you," snarked Aunt Christine.

"Uh, Bueller?" said Ezra into the phone. "I'm still here, you know."

"Sorry, honey," said Mom, sipping her martini. "Why don't you tell me what's going on, exactly?"

"Okay, so it's really strange, but for the last few days I've actually been able to hear myself talk," he said. "You know, like inside my head."

She sat silently for a few moments, confused, trying to make sense of what he had just said.

"Uh, hello, Mom? Are you still there?" he asked, expectantly.

"Yes, I'm here," she answered. "I'm just not quite sure how I'm supposed to respond to that information. Could you maybe be a little more specific?"

"It's like my ears are plugged, but they're not," he said. "Like my head is hollow."

"Don't let Beau hear you say something like that," I muttered to myself.

"Again, Ezra, a little more description would be helpful," pressed Mom.

"Look, I don't exactly know how to describe it, okay?" he huffed. "All I know is that it's weird and I don't like it."

"Okay, not a problem," she said calmly. "Has this been happening consistently?"

"No, just sometimes here lately," he said. "It kind of comes and goes."

"You know, I actually get that a lot whenever I play soccer," I said, stirring sweetener into my tea. "It usually happens whenever I overexert myself too much; I'm sure it'll go away in time."

"Did you hear your sister?" asked Mom. "She gets that too, sometimes."

"Yeah, but I'm not playing soccer," he countered. "And it happens when I'm not doing anything."

"Hmm, okay, well, let me ask you this, then," she said pointedly. "Have you been cleaning out your ears regularly?"

"Not recently, no," he said, slowly.

"And how long is 'not recently,' exactly?" asked Mom.

"I don't know, three or four months?" he said dismissively.

"Ezra, that's disgusting!" she shrieked. "You need to be cleaning out your ears regularly; you know this. You're twenty-one years old, for Christ's sake. Don't you think you should take more interest in your personal hygiene?"

"Okay, fine, I'll clean them!" he cried out defensively. "Geez, you don't have to get so angry."

She paused briefly to gather her patience. "Alright, listen, I'm fairly certain that not cleaning your ears out is what's causing the problem, so why don't you clean them and then see what happens."

"Okay, fine," he capitulated. "But will you at least still check out my ears when you get home? I really don't want to go deaf."

"You're not going to go deaf, Ezra,' she sighed. "But yes, if it will make you feel better, I will check them out once I get home. It may be a little while, but I promise I will."

"I probably won't be able to hear by then, so if you'd be so kind as to just tap me on the shoulder and alert me to your presence, that'd be great," he said, sarcastically.

"Goodbye, Ezra," said Mom, hanging up the phone.

"Well, that was interesting," drawled Aunt Christine.

"Ugh, how has this become my life?" sighed Mom.

"Better you than me, dear," chirped Grandma Helen. "I simply don't have the patience to deal with all of that."

Mom looked up just in time to see Justin walking by our table. "Justin, may we have another round of martinis, please?"

"Of course, you may," he answered exuberantly.

"Well, well, well, look who's going for round two," teased Grandma Helen. She smirked slyly over her martini glass before adding, "Of course, you may want to think about making it three. Lord knows what other catastrophes are awaiting you at home."

CHAPTER NINE

"Hi, honey, we're home," said Mom, walking through the back door. She placed her purse on the kitchen counter and made her way into the living room. "Have you and the boys had dinner?"

"We have, yes," said Dad, pressing the pause button on the remote. "Of course, Beau wasn't thrilled with the idea of leftover meatloaf, but he seemed to be able to fight through the agony." He gave her a wry smile. "So, how was dress shopping? Was it everything you dreamed it would be, and more?"

"Oh, it was definitely more, that's for sure," she said, plopping down onto the couch. "In fact, I think it may have been a little too much."

"Your mother was with you; of course, it was," he snickered. "So who did she upset this time?"

"Other than Christine, Addie, and myself?" said Mom. "Surprisingly, no one. Although I'm fairly certain she turned the poor girl that was helping us into an alcoholic, seeing as she immediately started chugging the leftover champagne as soon as we walked out the door."

"Waste not, want not. That's what I always say," he shrugged indifferently. "At least it was free."

"Hi Dad," I said, kissing him on the cheek. "What are you watching?"

"The US women's team is playing a friendly with Germany," he said, resuming the TV. "And it's scary, really, since the women on the German soccer team could seriously pass for the *Sons of Anarchy.* It's like watching a bunch of supermodels play against a band of burly marauders."

"I'm not so sure about that, Dad," I said doubtfully. "There are a few manly-looking women on the US team as well."

Dad paused the TV and pointed to one of the German defenders on the screen. "Tell me that woman doesn't look like a blonde Jason Momoa without the beard."

"Are we really even sure that's a woman?" asked Mom skeptically.

"I honestly couldn't tell you." He pressed the play button on the remote, and the game resumed. "But I'm pretty sure that half of these women could bench 315 pounds, easy. And that doesn't even include the goalie, who looks like she could give Lou Ferrigno a run for his money."

"Who?" I asked.

"Lou Ferrigno," he said. "You know, the guy who played the Incredible Hulk?"

"I thought that was CGI," I said, looking confused.

"I believe your father's referring to the person who played the original Hulk back in the seventies," said Mom. "The one that we used to watch when we were kids."

"Yeah, well, he's the only one, as far as I'm concerned," he mumbled irritably.

Mom leaned back and gestured toward the TV. "Well, Germany's size doesn't seem to be impeding the US any, seeing as they're winning 4-2 with less than a minute on the clock."

"Germany doesn't have the technical skills necessary to beat the US," said Dad, shaking his head. "And their whole 'kick the ball up the field' mentality isn't really working since they don't have anyone up front that can win it out of the air. So, other than knocking our girls down every chance they get, they really don't have much of a game plan."

"You know," said Mom, whispering in my ear. "This may be a good time to tell your father that you don't want to play soccer in college."

"I'll do it later," I said. "I don't want to interrupt the game."

"There are only thirty seconds left, Adelaide," she said pointedly. "Stop procrastinating."

"Can't you just do it for me?" I begged quietly.

"No, I can't. It's not my responsibility to tell him; it's yours." She softened her voice and then added, "Just be honest and tell him how you feel. I promise you'll feel better after you do."

"Okay, what's going on?" asked Dad, turning off the TV. "I know whenever the two of you whisper back and forth like that, it's either some sort of secret, or something you need to tell me, so you may as well just come out with it."

"Go on, honey," encouraged Mom quietly. "It's going to be okay; I promise."

I sat there feeling sick to my stomach. It was hard enough telling my mom that I wanted to quit, but telling my dad was going to be even harder. He's always been my rock whenever it came to soccer. He was my greatest supporter and the one person I would always go to whenever I needed advice both on and off the field. He spent countless hours filming and editing game footage so that I had something to send to college coaches. He was the main reason I was able to earn such a great soccer scholarship. How in the world was I going to sit here and tell him that it was all for naught and that I no longer wanted to play?

"Dad, there's something I need to tell you," I said somberly. "I've already talked to Mom, but you need to hear this too."

"Pumpkin, what's wrong?" he asked worriedly.

"I don't want to play soccer anymore," I said softly, a tear rolling down my cheek.

"What do you mean you don't want to play soccer?" asked Dad. "I thought you were excited to play for KSU."

"I was, or at least, I thought I was," I said. "But over the past few months, I've come to realize that I want my college experience to be more than constant practices, training sessions, and travel. I want to experience college life outside of sports. I don't want all of my time to be tied up doing something I don't love anymore." Tears were streaming down my face at this point. I could barely breathe; I was so upset. "Please don't worry about the money," I sobbed. "My academic scholarships will more than cover everything other than my living—"

"Stop," said Dad, rising from his chair. He knelt down in front of me and pulled me close. "You don't need to say anymore, Addie. I love you, and I only want to see you happy. If that means quitting soccer, then so be it." He slowly pulled back and wiped away my tears. "You know your mother and I will always support you in any way that we can, so if you no longer want to play soccer, then that's fine with me."

"Yes, but I know how much money and time you've invested in me, and—"

"Shh, don't you worry about that," he said. "I'm certainly not."

"Yes, but I feel bad that you spent so much money," my voice cracking through the tears. "Club soccer, showcases, travel; it all cost so much!"

"Honey, look at me," he said, lifting my chin. "Your mother and I loved watching you play soccer because it made you happy. But if you're no longer happy, then there's no reason to keep doing it, is there?"

"No," I agreed, accepting a tissue from Mom to blow my nose. "I just don't want you to feel like you wasted a bunch of time and money on me, that's all," I sniffed. "And I don't want you to be disappointed in me."

"We did waste time and money," he chuckled softly. "But it was worth every penny to see you happy and thriving." He handed me another tissue so that I could wipe my eyes. "And you could never disappoint us."

"Yes, but—" I said.

"No buts," he interrupted, shaking his head. "You are an intelligent and amazing person who just happened to play soccer. It doesn't define who you are, and it never will."

"Your father's right, honey," said Mom. "We could never be disappointed in you. We love you, and we always will."

Dad handed me a clean tissue. "And we don't ever want you to feel like you can't come and tell us these things. Our job, as parents, is to always make sure that you have a place to come whenever you're uncertain about life. That you have someone to talk to who can help carry the burden, and this isn't something you should've carried alone, honey."

"I know," I nodded slowly. "I was just too scared to tell you, that's all."

"Don't ever be afraid to come to me, honey." He lovingly placed his hand on my cheek. "Remember, I can't help you if you don't tell me what's going on."

"I know, and I'm sorry," I said penitently. "I promise to be more upfront and transparent next time."

"I'd appreciate that." He stood and walked back over to his chair. "So, are there any other truth bombs the two of you are planning to drop on me tonight?"

"No, I think that pretty much covered it," said Mom, heaving a deep sigh. "Although I think I could use a glass of wine after that." She got up and headed toward the kitchen. "Can I get anyone else anything?"

"I'll take a bourbon, if you don't mind," said Dad.

"I'm good, thanks," I smiled wanly.

"Hey, everything's going to be okay," said Dad encouragingly. "You're not alone in this. We'll figure out a game plan and go from there, alright?"

"A game plan for what?" asked Beau, coming down the stairs.

"Your sister has decided to step away from soccer so that she can focus solely on her academics," said Dad. He then smiled and winked at me. "And we couldn't be prouder."

"Dang, that's a lot of money down the drain," drawled Beau. "Not to mention a really poor return on investment." He sat down on the ottoman in front of Dad's chair and crossed his arms. "So now I suppose we're going to have to pay for your education, yes?"

"We're?" asked Dad incredulously.

"Shut up, dork!" I yelled. "My academic scholarships are more than enough to cover everything, so just back off, okay?"

"Well, everything except for the dorm and meal plan," said Mom, handing Dad his bourbon. "Which, of course, is moot since you'll still be living here."

"What?" said Beau, jumping up. "You mean I'm still going to have to live with her?"

"It looks that way, swine boy," I smiled sweetly.

"I don't believe this!" exclaimed Beau, plopping back down. "Why can't we just pay for her to stay in the dorms?"

"Again, we?" asked Dad, raising his brow.

"Well, I, for one, am thrilled that your sister's going to continue living here," said Mom. "It helps balance out all the testosterone."

"Ugh, whatever," sighed Beau irritably. He stood and walked over to the back door, calling for Churchill to follow him. "Come on, buddy, it's time to release the Kraken."

"I'm sorry, what did you just say?" asked Dad.

"It's code for poop, Dad," he said. "Because I absolutely refuse to say, 'Let's go potty' like Mom does. It's so degrading."

"Degrading?" said Mom, her voice rising an octave. "I love that dog with all my heart!"

"Yes, but he doesn't appreciate being spoken to like a baby," he countered. "He's 35 years old in dog years and would like to be treated as such." He opened the door to let Churchill out. "I mean, would you have wanted someone talking to you like that when you were his age? I think not!"

"I can't even believe we're having this discussion," said Mom, wearily. "But by all means, continue on. I would hate for Churchill to hold off releasing the Kraken on my account."

Just then, Ezra came downstairs and stared accusingly at Mom. "I thought you said you were going to look at my ears as soon as you got home."

"Oh, honey, I'm sorry, I completely forgot," she apologized. "I'll be right up."

"Oh, so now all of a sudden you actually care that I might be going deaf?" he asked.

"You are not going deaf, Ezra," she said irritably. "We already went over this."

"Yes, but the fact remains that you still completely forgot about me," he retorted sourly.

"Honey, again, I apologize." She stood and walked over to him. "Did you clean your ears like I asked?"

"Yes," he nodded.

"Do you think it helped?" she asked.

"I think so, yes," he answered. "I'd still feel better if you looked at them, though."

"Okay," she said. "Come with me into the kitchen and I'll take a look."

"Have I missed something?" asked Dad, looking confused.

"Ezra thinks he's going deaf," I said. "Oh, and you should probably know that Beau thinks he's going blind."

"I'm sorry, what?" he asked. "How am I just finding out about this?"

"Don't worry, nine times out of ten it ends up being nothing," I said dismissively. "But the minute Mom plays into it, they act like they're dying."

"Don't they do that already?" asked Dad sarcastically.

We watched as Mom finished inspecting both of Ezra's ears with a penlight.

"Everything looks perfectly fine to me," she said, putting the light away. "But we can certainly revisit it in a few days, if you'd like."

"Unless you forget about me again," he glowered.

"I promise I won't," she chuckled. "I'll even put it on my calendar."

"Thanks, Mom," he smiled, hugging her tightly.

"You're welcome, baby," she said, hugging him back.

"Oh, and just so you know, I'm still only giving you 2.5 stars on Yelp," he snarked, running up the back stairs. "People have a right to be informed, Mom!"

"You know, I really don't get paid enough for everything I have to put up with," she sighed, picking up her wine glass.

Mom was coming out of the kitchen just as Beau and Churchill were walking back into the house.

"I meant to ask you earlier, honey," she said. "How are your eyes doing? Are you still seeing flashes of light?"

"Oh yeah, I forgot to tell you," he said, reaching for the wipe warmer. "I'm actually fine. It turns out those bright spots were just fireflies flying around me."

"You can't possibly be serious," said Mom incredulously.

"No, really, that's exactly what they were," he nodded excitedly.

She watched as he cleaned Churchill's backside. "Son, how could you not know that those were fireflies? They're out every summer; you're well acquainted with them."

"Well, excuse me for never seeing a white firefly before!" he snapped, throwing the wipe away and washing his hands. "They've always been yellow in the past. Maybe they're some sort of mutant firefly or something, I don't know."

"Mutant fireflies," said Mom, walking over to the couch. "That's a new one." She sat down next to me and quietly sipped her wine. "Okay, well, I think I've had all the excitement I can handle today."

"I guess this probably isn't the best time to tell you that my mother wants to throw a paint-by-numbers bridal luncheon for Christine, is it?" asked Dad uneasily.

"What?" shrieked Mom.

"And that she wants you to come over tomorrow to discuss it," he added quickly.

"Greg, no," she said, her shoulders sagging. "That's a terrible idea."

"I know," he said calmly, trying to placate her. "But maybe just hear her out, okay?"

"Can you see my mother and Nancy sitting down to do a paint-by-numbers?"

"Look, I think Mom just wants to do something nice for Christine," said Dad. "You know how much she adores her." He stood and held out his hand for her empty glass. "Why don't I go ahead and pour you what's left of that wine, and we'll discuss it, okay?"

Mom glared silently up at him.

"Correction," he chuckled. "Why don't I pour you what's left of that wine and then open another bottle, and we'll discuss it?"

"Fine," she sighed heavily, handing him her glass. "But you may want to prepare your mother for what she's signing up for."

"Nah," he said with a wink, "That's why I have you."

CHAPTER TEN

The next morning, I came downstairs to find Mom and Aunt Christine drinking coffee and discussing Nana's offer to host her a painting themed bridal luncheon.

"It's a disaster waiting to happen, Chrissy," said Mom.

"Oh come on, what's the worst that can happen?" she asked. "We'll paint for a few hours, snack on some hors d' oeuvres, and drink a lot of wine. I think it'll be fun."

"I agree with Aunt Christine, Mom," I said, pouring myself a cup of coffee. "It'll be like our own little paint and sip."

"Well, let's just hope your grandmother doesn't throw her usual tantrum," said Mom. "You know how much she abhors anything crafty."

"Oh, please, one afternoon isn't going to kill her," dismissed Aunt Christine. "Besides, I'm actually kind of excited about it. It was sweet of Carol to come up with the idea. I really appreciate her wanting to play a part in the wedding."

"Well, you can tell her that this afternoon," said Mom. "We need to swing by there on the way to the florist because she wants to discuss the details."

"Ugh, can't you just do it?" whined Aunt Christine. "I have so much on my plate as it is, and I don't want to be late to meet Christian."

"Oh no, you don't," said Mom, shaking her head. "I don't feel like being sucked into the vortex that is Carol today, so you and Addie are both going to go with me. That way, I have an excuse to leave early." She slowly sipped her coffee and then looked at Aunt Christine in confusion. "Wait, who's Christian?

"He's the wedding planner," she answered. "I thought I told you about him."

"If you did, I honestly don't remember," said Mom. "Of course, that's not surprising considering all that's been going on lately." She reached for the coffee pot and refilled her cup. "So, how did you hear about him?"

"Marjorie Nichols recommended him," she said. "I ran into her a few months ago when I was getting my brakes fixed, and she gave me his card. He helped with her daughter's wedding and said that he came highly recommended, so I called him. It's a good thing I did, too, because one of the weddings he was planning had just been called off, and he was able to work me in. And, since we already have the venue figured out, he really only needs to help with the flowers, the wedding cake, and the caterers. Oh, and I think he's planning to come to the wine tasting as well."

"He sounds great," smiled Mom. "I look forward to meeting him."

"Apparently, you already have," said Aunt Christine. "He says he went to high school with you."

"He did?" asked Mom. "What's his last name?"

"Lacroix," she answered. "Christian Lacroix."

"I don't remember a Christian Lacroix," said Mom, folding her arms. "There was a Christian Latimer in my English class, but I don't remember anyone with the last name Lacroix."

"Well, maybe you'll remember when you see him," she shrugged.

"See who?" asked Dad, coming into the kitchen.

"A guy named Christian Lacroix," said Mom. "He's Christine's wedding planner and someone I apparently went to high school with, but I don't recognize the name. I guess I'll find out when we go to the florist later today."

"Are you still planning on swinging by my parents' house?" he asked, opening the refrigerator. "Mom's really looking forward to discussing the luncheon."

"Yes, honey, I know," acquiesced Mom. "We'll be leaving here shortly."

"Okay, good. I told her you'd be—" He let out an irritable growl and picked up a container of leftovers. "Alright, who keeps putting the small containers on the bottom shelf? "I've told everyone to stop doing that."

"Is it really that big of a deal, Greg?" sighed Mom.

"Yes, it is," he snapped, pulling out multiple containers. "It makes it harder to reach the things that keep getting pushed back, like my flavored coffee creamer. I either have to pull everything out like I am now, or risk having it dumped out all over the floor. It's irritating and it needs to stop!"

"You know, I highly doubt Gary would get angry about something like that," said Mom, handing him a fresh cup of coffee. "In fact, he'd probably be a lot more understanding and nicer about it, too. He's not really the temperamental type."

"That's not getting any funnier, Olivia," he snarled, pouring creamer into his coffee.

"Oh, come on, I'm only kidding," she chuckled. "You know I only have eyes for you."

"Yeah, well, the joke's getting old," he answered testily. He placed the creamer back into the refrigerator and headed toward his office. "I have to get back to work."

"What was that all about?" asked Aunt Christine.

"And who's Gary?" I added.

"A few weeks ago, your father had a dream that I divorced him and immediately remarried some guy named Gary. Now whenever he gets irritated, I just tell him that Gary would be a lot calmer, understanding, and would probably never get mad about something so trivial." She gave us a wicked grin. "I know I should stop, but it's just been so much fun antagonizing him."

"You're evil," I said pointedly.

"Oh, believe me, honey, your father gives back just as good as he gets," countered Mom.

"Hmm, that must make things interesting," smiled Aunt Christine mischievously.

"We've definitely had our moments, that's for sure," she winked.

"Ew, gross!" I shuddered. "You're talking about my dad!"

"Addie, how exactly do you think you got here?" asked Mom. "It certainly wasn't by immaculate conception."

"Alright, my darlings, I'm here!" exclaimed Grandma Helen, walking through the back door. "Let's go wine tasting!"

"That's not until Friday, Mom," said Aunt Christine.

"What?" she shrieked. "I thought that was today. I cleared my schedule and everything."

"Tell me, Mother, have you even taken the time to consult the agenda I printed up for you?" asked Mom. "It has all the dates, days, and times of everything we need to do, so there is absolutely no reason for you not to be aware of what is happening."

"Oh, I'm sure it's in the house somewhere," she said dismissively. "I'll eventually find it."

"Well, it may behoove you to find it sooner rather than later," said Mom. "That way there won't be any surprises."

"But I love surprises!" exclaimed Grandma Helen jubilantly. "They're always so fun and unexpected." She sat down next to Aunt Christine and me. "Okay, so if we're not planning on tasting wine, what is it that we're doing, exactly?"

"Flowers," said Mom.

"Ugh, flowers sound boring," she said petulantly.

"We're also going to swing by Carol's house to discuss a few things," added Aunt Christine.

"Ugh, that sounds even worse," she snarled.

"You know, we're perfectly capable of doing all of this without you," said Mom, raising her brow.

"Oh, don't be ridiculous, Olivia," she scoffed. "I have every intention of helping the two of you plan this wedding, even though you booked that god awful venue behind my back."

"Don't even start, Mother," said Aunt Christine, raising her hand in warning.

"Well, I'm sorry, but I just don't understand the allure of having a wedding on a farm. It's so rural and inelegant," said Grandma Helen, ignoring the warning. "I can practically hear the incessant banjo music playing right now."

"The Laurel Estate is an absolutely beautiful property, Grandma," I said. "My friend's sister was married there, and the scenery is absolutely gorgeous. It'll make the perfect backdrop for a fall wedding."

"Yes, but must it take place outside?" she groaned. "It is, after all, still a farm."

"It's not like that, Mother, and you know it," said Mom pointedly. We're not talking about factory farming. It's an upscale equestrian property with stables and polo fields, for God's sake. You'll be well within your element."

"Not to mention, the only thing actually taking place outside is the ceremony," added Aunt Christine. "The reception will be held inside a lavish event hall with every modern convenience you could possibly want, so stop acting like I'm getting married in the middle of *Deliverance* country amongst a slew of tractors and backhoes. It's insulting."

"Okay, fine, I'll stop," said Grandma Helen defensively. "There's no need to get angry, darling."

"Thank you," muttered Aunt Christine.

"So, why is it that we need to stop by Carol's house?" she asked, changing the subject.

"She wants to discuss the details of Chrissy's bridal luncheon," answered Mom.

"Carol's planning your bridal luncheon?" she queried. "When was this decided?"

"We only found out about it yesterday," said Mom. "She told Greg that she wanted to do something nice for Christine and help take some of the pressure off of the wedding planning. I think it's her way of being able to play a small part in all of this."

"I see," said Grandma Helen. "Well then, it's a good thing I'm coming with you today. Now I'll be able to run interference and stop any tacky ideas from surfacing. Lord only knows what's going on in that woman's mind."

"Yeah, about that," said Mom hesitantly. "She's apparently already decided on a theme and is planning on hosting the luncheon at her house."

"Why her house?" demanded Grandma Helen. "And why hasn't she discussed any of this with me? I thought we were friends."

"Friends?" drawled Aunt Christine sarcastically. "You can't possibly be serious."

"Alright, fine, I'm using the term loosely, but you know what I mean," admitted Grandma Helen, before turning her attention back to Mom. "Okay, so what kind of theme is it, and how unhappy am I going to be about it?"

"She's planning Chrissy a paint-by-numbers party," answered Mom.

"She's what?" she shrieked. "And you agreed to this?"

"I think it sounds fun, Grandma," I said.

"So do I, Addie," agreed Aunt Christine.

"No," Grandma Helen said, shaking her head vehemently. "Fun is making multiple trips back-and-forth to Dante's Bloody Mary bar, where there are over 150 garnishes and 25 vodkas to choose from. It is not slathering cheap paint over a canvas of numbers."

"Uh, as I recall, Dad had to pour you into the car and hand you a paper sack to throw up in after your afternoon at Dante's," said Mom.

"Must you always focus on the negative, Olivia?" she snarled. "Listen, I say we change the venue to Dante's. That way you can all still do your painting and I'll have Bloody Mary's to keep me occupied."

"I'm sorry, Mom, but I just don't think that's going to work," said Mom, shaking her head. "Carol operates classes out of her house, so having to transport all of her supplies and easels is going to be a tremendous hassle, and a lot to ask."

"Plus, Nana loves throwing parties," I said. "It makes her happy."

"Ugh, that woman is such a simpleton," mumbled Grandma Helen irritably. "I still can't believe you married into that family."

"Please play nice, Mother," said Mom. "And that family you're referencing is the reason I'm sane and you're still alive. If I didn't have Greg to offset the craziness of you, I'd honestly be residing in a jail cell right now."

"Well, well, well, aren't we pithy?" she snarked.

"I tell you what," interrupted Aunt Christine. "Why don't we let Carol plan the Bridal luncheon, and you can plan the bachelorette party. That way, everyone can be involved."

"Yes!" exclaimed Grandma Helen excitedly. "Oh, Christine, I have so many ideas!"

"I'm sure you do, but unfortunately, that discussion is going to have to wait," said Mom. "We're going to have to leave soon if we're going to make it to Carol's on time."

"Ugh, can't we just FaceTime her from here?" asked Grandma Helen. "I'm just not in the mood for sappy southern charm today."

"Carol specifically asked us to stop by, and that is exactly what we are going to do," said Mom, rifling through her purse. "Has anyone seen my phone? I need to call Beau and remind him to take Mrs. Schmidt's trash out to the curb today."

She started to look around the kitchen and then remembered she had left it in the car. "Addie, honey, do you mind if I borrow your phone?" she asked. "I think I left mine in the car."

"Sure,' I said, handing her the phone. "You just need to press the button and say, "Call Butthead."

"Okay, that is not very nice," she admonished. "You're going to need to change that." She then pushed down the button and rolled her eyes. "Call Butthead."

"What do you want?" barked Beau rudely into the phone. "I'm busy!"

"This is your mother," snapped Mom.

"Oh, sorry, Mom," he answered penitently. "I thought it was Addie calling."

"Tell me, is there some reason you can't be civil toward your sister whenever she calls you? She may be alerting you to an emergency or trying to save your life; you have absolutely no idea, so stop being rude. It's completely uncalled for."

"Yes, ma'am," he said.

"Now listen, have you taken Mrs. Schmidt's trash to the curb yet?" she asked.

"No, not yet, but I will."

"Well, don't forget," said Mom. "She's paying you to do that while she's out of town."

"Yes, ma'am, I know."

"I'm heading out for most of the day, but if you need me, call me. I love you." She ended the call and then handed the phone back to me. "You have my full permission to keep his name the way you have it."

Chapter Eleven

"Hey y'all!" exclaimed Nana, opening the back door. She hugged each one of us in turn and then led us into the kitchen. "I'm so glad y'all could stop by today. I've been working in the kitchen all morning making your favorite things!"

"Carol, you didn't have to do that," said Mom.

"Oh, please, I was happy to do it," she drawled. She gestured toward the kitchen table. "Addie, honey, I know how much you love my pepper jelly dip, so please, go ahead and dig in. Olivia, I made sure to make a special batch of pimento cheese with jalapenos just for you, and Christine, I made your favorite chess squares, so y'all don't be shy, grab a plate, and fill it up!"

"Ollie's right, Carol, you didn't have to go to all this trouble," smiled Aunt Christine.

"Well, I know how busy y'all are with the wedding planning, and I'm sure my asking all of you to swing by out of the blue probably didn't help any, so I thought the least I could do was feed you while we discussed things." Nana then turned her attention toward Grandma Helen. "And had I known you were coming, Helen, I would have made you those grape jelly meatballs you love so much."

"Oh, yes, those meatballs are fabulous!" enthused Grandma Helen. "I keep hoping you'll break down and share the recipe with me one of these days."

"Alright, let's try not going too over the top, Mother," muttered Mom. "She may just pop into the kitchen and start making you some."

It's no secret in our family that Nana is the complete antithesis of Grandma Helen. Where Grandma Helen loves to shop, drink, and make fun of people, Nana loves to garden, paint, and feed everyone who comes through her door. Unfortunately for Grandma Helen, this primarily consists of an abundance of southern comfort cuisine, which according to her, is the equivalent of consuming a plate full of, and I quote, "insipid and unpalatable garbage."

Of course, over the years, Mom has forbidden her to ever say any of this to Nana, so to keep the peace, she has spent the last 23 years hyperbolizing her love for southern cuisine and pretty much blatantly lying through her teeth. Because when it comes down to it, Grandma Helen detests those grape jelly meatballs and literally rues the day that they were introduced to her.

"Now, now, it's a secret, Helen, you know that," winked Nana. "But I tell you what, the next time you come over, I'll be sure to make a great big batch just for you!"

"That's it, I'm never coming over here again, Olivia," she hissed.

Nana waited for us all to sit down and then offered us something to drink.

"I just made some fresh lemonade from the lemons in my garden. Can I get y'all a glass?"

"I don't suppose you happen to have anything stronger?" asked Grandma Helen. "It's been a bit of a morning already, if you know what I mean."

"Oh, yes, of course I do," she answered congenially. "I'll just go into the kitchen and brew some coffee. I even have some of that Almond Cherry Macaron creamer that's been selling out at the Piggly Wiggly."

"Uh, I was thinking more along the lines of vodka, dear," she clarified. "Perhaps even a vodka and soda."

"Oh, heavens, no," said Nana, shaking her head. "That's a bit too much for me." She opened the refrigerator door and peered into it. "Although I think I may still have some of that muscadine wine George bought me for Valentine's Day in here somewhere."

"Oh, dear God, that's not wine, that's undrinkable swill!" whispered Grandma Helen.

"Lemonade will be great, Carol, thanks," smiled Mom. She then turned toward Grandma Helen and lowered her voice. "Mother, if you don't stop being obnoxious, I'm going to specifically request that those grape jelly meatballs be served at the wedding."

"You wouldn't dare!" she hissed.

"Watch me," glowered Mom.

"Okay, fine, I'll be nice," she conceded. "But what am I supposed to drink in the meantime?"

"You will drink the lemonade and you will like it," said Mom.

Nana set down a tray with a pitcher of lemonade and five glasses. "You know, I just can't tell y'all how much it means to me to be able to throw this bridal luncheon for you, Christine. I was honestly worried you might be a little upset, considering I'm not a close family member."

"I've always considered you to be close family, Carol," smiled Aunt Christine. She reached out and squeezed Nana's hand softly. "And the fact that you offered to do this means the world to me, I hope you know that."

"Well, it just kind of struck me the other day that a paint-by-numbers bridal luncheon might be something that you'd enjoy," smiled Nana.

"Too bad that's the only thing that struck you," muttered Grandma Helen.

"Stop or I will kill you," mouthed Mom.

"To be completely honest, I actually got the idea after a young bride had booked one of my classes for her and her bridesmaid's last weekend. They all had so much fun, and so I thought, why not offer this to Christine?" She took a sip of lemonade. "Plus, with everything else you have going on, I thought this might make things a little bit easier for you."

"I'm fairly certain we would have managed, somehow," said Grandma Helen sweetly.

"Well, I think it's a fantastic idea!" exclaimed Aunt Christine. "And I'm really looking forward to it."

"You know, Carol," interjected Grandma Helen. "I was actually thinking we might do all of this at Dante's. They have an absolutely phenomenal Bloody Mary bar that is just to die for, and they even have a private back room that will accommodate all of us. I've spoken to Dante, and he is more than willing to set something up. We just need to set a date."

"And when, exactly, did you do that?" asked Mom incredulously. "I only told you about this an hour ago."

"Oh, I texted him on the ride over here," she beamed. "You know how much he adores me."

"That's not the point, Mother," said Mom irritably. "I specifically told you that Dante's was not a good idea."

"Did you?" she asked innocently. "I honestly don't remember. I think I was just so excited about the idea of a paint-by-numbers bridal luncheon that I must have completely blocked it out." She then turned her attention over to Nana. "Carol, you absolutely must let me help you with this luncheon. An afternoon filled with painting and Bloody Mary's sounds absolutely delightful, don't you think?"

"Mom, this was Carol's idea," said Aunt Christine. "Why don't we let her do what she wants to do?"

"And that's exactly what I'm doing, darling," she said enthusiastically. "Carol will take care of the painting while I handle all the food and drinks. And, having it at Dante's will alleviate the stress of having to cook, clean, and host the event."

"Well—" started Nana.

"And, you won't have to clean up after everyone," interrupted Grandma Helen. "Nor will you have to kick George out of the house. It's really a win-win for everyone!"

"Well, I suppose that could work," said Nana uneasily.

"Carol, we are more than happy to have the luncheon here, if that's easier on you," interjected Mom. "Please don't feel pressured into having it at Dante's if that's not what you really want."

"No one's pressuring her, darling," scoffed Grandma Helen. "I'm simply trying to make things easier for her." She looked over at Nana. "And I know that transferring all of your supplies may be a bit of a task, so I'll enlist the help of Ezra and Beau to help transport it all."

"Is that so?" asked Mom. "I hope you're planning on paying them for their time."

"I'm their grandmother, they'll be more than happy to help me," she smiled confidently. "And yes, I'll pay them."

"Well, I suppose that would make things a lot easier for me," said Nana. "Are you sure you don't mind helping me with all of this, Helen? I know I kind of sprung it on everyone."

"Darling, the fact that you are willing to go out of your way to do something so kind for my precious Christine means so much to me," she cooed. "And I would never forgive myself if I allowed you to carry the burden alone. So please, let me help you."

"Having the luncheon at Dante's does sound like it'll be a lot of fun," said Nana. "And if the boys are willing to help me transport everything to and from the restaurant, I think it could work."

"Well then, it's settled, painting and Bloody Mary's at Dante's!" exclaimed Grandma Helen. "I'll call and make the reservation right now."

***

"You should be absolutely ashamed of yourself, Mother!" said Mom, angrily pulling out of Nana and Pop's driveway. "That poor woman actually believes you want to help her with this bridal luncheon when all you really want is a damn Bloody Mary bar!" She glared back at Grandma Helen in the rearview mirror. "You know, every time I think you've hit a new low, you actually go and one-up it."

"Ollie's right, Mom," agreed Aunt Christine. "You seriously take selfishness to a whole new level."

"Oh, please," she said, crossing her arms in defiance. "I didn't force her hand into anything, I simply helped guide her into making a better decision, that's all."

"Still, it was kind of a low blow, Grandma," I said softly.

"Oh, so you want to weigh in now, too?" she snapped, raising her brow.

"Addie's right, it was a low blow," agreed Mom. "And let's not forget how you completely disregarded what I said earlier about Dante's not being the best place to have the luncheon. That was completely underhanded and you know it."

"I don't understand why all of you are getting so upset," she said defensively. "Carol is in complete agreement with me, for God's sake!"

"Yes, after you manipulated her into thinking that you actually cared about helping her," answered Aunt Christine. "Seriously, Mother, I can't believe you did that."

"I can," muttered Mom. "She does it all the time."

The car fell silent while Grandma Helen reflected on everything that had been said. She heaved a heavy sigh and looked sullenly out the window as we made our way across town to make our appointment with Christian and the florist.

"Okay, fine, maybe it wasn't my finest hour," she relented.

"You think?" asked Mom sarcastically.

"Isn't that what I just said?" she shot back irritably.

Aunt Christine shifted herself around in the front seat to look back at Grandma Helen. "Look, I understand that you're not the biggest fan of Carol's lifestyle, but sometimes you come off a bit harsh whenever you're around her."

"A bit?" repeated Mom.

"I've got this, Olivia, thank you," said Aunt Christine irritably. Returning her attention to Grandma Helen, she continued. "As I was saying, you treat her harshly, and I think a lot of her unanimity is a result of wanting to please you. I don't think you realize the kind of clout you carry with her. She respects you and cares about what you think."

"Which is a complete mystery to me," mumbled Mom.

"Anyway," continued Aunt Christine. "You may want to think about showing a little more kindness toward Carol, especially since she considers you her friend."

Aunt Christine was right. Nana has always been a good friend to Grandma Helen, even when it hasn't been reciprocated. And try as she may, Nana just can't seem to make a connection with her. Of course, what she doesn't know is that Grandma Helen prides herself on allowing very few people into her inner circle. Outside of her own family, she tends to push people away, either through sarcasm, unwarranted judgement or just plain aggression. Maybe it's some sort of coping mechanism, I really don't know. But whatever it is, I hope she eventually lets her in, because Nana is a great person to have in your corner.

"Perhaps you're right," said Grandma Helen defeatedly. "Maybe I am a bit insensitive when it comes to Carol."

"You know, you may want to think about giving her a call and apologizing," said Mom.

"I suppose I can do that," she sighed. "But I've already locked in the reservation at Dante's, and if we cancel, we'll lose our deposit."

"No one's asking you to cancel it, Mom," said Aunt Christine. "But maybe just give her a call and ask her to lunch; that way you can both plan everything together."

"Yes, that's what I'll do!" exclaimed Grandma Helen happily. "I'll take her to lunch and spend some time with her. Maybe we'll even go shopping!"

"I think she'd really appreciate that," smiled Mom.

"Wonderful, I'll call her tonight," she trilled, pulling out her compact. "But I would like to point out that we all dodged a bullet back there."

"What do you mean, Grandma?" I asked.

"Darling, had I not intervened, we very well may have been dining on crawdads, collard greens, and deep-fried oysters," she said, curling her lip. "I may be able to look past some things, but southern, down-home cooking is where I draw the line."

"Well, her benevolence was fun while it lasted," snarked Mom.

Chapter Twelve

Walking through the front door of Petal & Stem, a local floral boutique in the heart of downtown Canton, was like walking into an enchanting world full of vibrant color and old-world charm. Large wooden shelves and rustic crates, decorated in white, twinkling lights were filled with hand-tied bouquets, bright floral arrangements, and charming gift baskets, while galvanized, vintage buckets overflowing with various types of flowers such as tulips, lilies, hydrangeas, and sunflowers, lie scattered across the floor.

Making my way further into the store, I could smell the sweet scent of rose, lavender, and eucalyptus permeating the air, while the soft sound of trickling water from a nearby fountain lent a spa-like feel to the large, efflorescent space.

"Ooh, a fountain!" exclaimed Grandma Helen. "Addie, do you have a penny? I want to make a wish!"

"Uh, I don't think it's that kind of fountain, Grandma," I said, peering down into the bottom. "There aren't any coins in there."

"Well, that's no fun," she retorted. "What's the point in having a fountain, then?"

"Probably because it adds a soothing background for people while they shop," I said.

"It's a flower shop, how much more soothing can you get?" Taking a deep breath, she crossed her arms and focused her attention on Mom and Aunt Christine, who were still slowly browsing the front of the store. "Ugh, this is going to take forever."

"Well, they can't take too long," I said, looking at my phone. "Their appointment is in five minutes."

As we continued making our way toward the back of the store, we overheard the boisterous voice of a man discussing the nightmare of having to deal with one of his recent brides-to-be.

"So I said, don't be daft, Daphne, carnations have absolutely no business being in a bridal bouquet," said the voice. "Now, if you're planning to get married in some godforsaken place like Bucksnort, Tennessee, you might be able to get away with that, but here in the metro Atlanta area, carnations are very much frowned upon."

"Bucksnort, Tennessee?" came a woman's voice. "Is that even a real place, or did you just make it up?"

"Oh, it's a very real place, Renee," answered the man. "And it looks even more rural than it sounds." He paused to take a sip of his Starbucks Frappuccino and then continued with his story. "Anyway, I practically lost my lunch after that conversation. I mean, what kind of person suggests adding carnations to their bridal arrangement? It's absolutely inane."

"Well, considering the carnation is both a dull and incredibly unsightly flower, I would venture to say someone who is unimaginative, uninspiring, and completely bromidic," said Grandma Helen, perusing a shelf of notecards. "A simpleton, if you will."

The man turned around and arched his brow. "I'm sorry, who are you?"

"Helen Vitali, mother of the bride," she smiled primly.

"Well, Helen," he drawled her name out slowly and then immediately followed with a devilish grin. "That has got to be one of the best things I've heard all day. And you're right, by the way, she's definitely all four of those things." Taking her hand in his, he bowed slightly and kissed her hand. "Christian Lacroix, wedding consultant, at your service."

"Mother, I thought you said you were going to wait for us," said Aunt Christine, stepping up behind Grandma Helen. "We turned around, and you both were gone."

"Yes, well, we got bored," she sighed. "And with the two of you taking so long, Addie and I decided to set our sights on something a little more interesting." She turned and smiled up at Christian. "And believe me, you are so much more interesting, darling. So, tell me, were you able to foil the whole carnation catastrophe from happening?"

"Thank the good Lord in Heaven, yes!" he exclaimed dramatically. "Can you imagine if I hadn't? My reputation would have been ruined." He placed his arm around Aunt Christine. "Thankfully, I'm not going to have to worry about any of that with Christine because she has exceptional taste."

"A trait, I'm proud to say, that she inherited from me," smiled Grandma Helen self-satisfactorily. "Of course, I still see a bit of my husband in her from time to time, but that really can't be helped, I suppose."

"Oh, you're a lively one, aren't you?" winked Christian. "I can already tell that you and I are going to be fast friends." He glanced over at Aunt Christine. "Christine, your mother is an absolute gem. I'm so glad you brought her here today."

As the three of us stood listening to Christian share his recent ideas regarding the colors for the floral arrangements, Mom irritably walked up and said, "Well, thanks a lot for telling me where everyone went off to."

"Oh, my God, Olivia, is that you?" exclaimed Christian, holding out his arms. "You look absolutely amazing!"

"Christian!" she responded, stepping into his embrace. "It's so good to see you. Chrissy mentioned that you said we'd gone to high school together, but I thought your last name was Latimer."

"It's Lacroix now," he said. "I always hated the name Latimer; it always sounded so pedestrian and uninteresting. I needed something with a little more flair if I ever planned to sell myself as a top-notch wedding consultant. Anyway, after living in LA for a while, I decided to move back after Mama died. Eventually, I bought a house, opened my own wedding event company, and voila, here we are."

"I'm so sorry to hear about your mother, Christian," said Mom. "I had no idea that she had passed."

"Breast cancer, five years ago," he sighed. "Dad didn't take it very well, but ever since he's moved into the Magnolia House, he seems to have a little more pep in his step. I think he's finally turned a corner and is learning to live life again. He loves playing Bingo with his friends and has recently taken up gardening and painting, which is honestly something I never thought I'd see him do."

"That's wonderful, Christian," said Mom. "I've heard nothing but great things about Magnolia House. A few of my friends' parents live there, and they absolutely love it."

"It was honestly the best decision I could have made for him," said Christian. "He was so lonely and sad after Mom died; it just broke my heart."

Clapping his hands together, he immediately changed the subject. "Anyway, enough with all of this sad talk, we have a wedding to plan, remember?"

"Olivia," hissed Grandma Helen, pulling Mom close. "Don't you dare even entertain that thought. I can already see the wheels turning inside that head of yours."

"Have you gone completely mental?" she said. "What are you talking about?"

"Shoving your father and me into that home," she said, squeezing her arm tightly.

"Ouch, that hurts!" exclaimed Mom, breaking away from her grip. "And that never even entered my mind, although I'm starting to warm up to the idea now."

"I'm serious, Olivia," she said, crossing her arms in defiance. "I absolutely refuse to live in one of those places."

"And you're not going to," said Mom, rubbing the circulation back into her arm. "Besides, I could never do something like that to Dad; he's a good man and deserves better." She absently picked up a scented candle and held it to her nose. "And, since your wagon's hitched to his, you're pretty much safe."

"Why must you always say things to hurt me, dear?" she sighed.

"Because you usually have it coming." She pointed to her sore arm and then added, "And because you have a tendency to be violent."

"I'm sorry, I didn't mean to hurt you," said Grandma Helen penitently. "I just don't want to be discarded like I don't matter; like I'm used goods and have nothing to offer the world." She looked up at Mom with sadness in her eyes. "I know what places like that can do to people, Olivia. They suck the life out of you until you become the shell of your former self and have no idea how to live anymore. You just eat, sleep, and wait for death."

"Okay, first of all, let's tone down the drama some, alright?" said Mom. "And secondly, Magnolia House is actually a lovely place for seniors to live. They offer a lot of fun activities like gardening, dance lessons, trivia nights, and bingo. In fact, my friend Michele's mom lives there and absolutely loves it. She's recently taken up scrapbooking and is now making memory books for all of her grandkids."

"Ugh, that sounds absolutely dreadful," she shuddered.

"Yeah, well, maybe to you, but not to most people," replied Mom. "Where is all of this coming from, anyway?"

"I don't know," she sighed. "I guess I'm just worried that you're eventually going to get tired of dealing with me, and I'm going to end up in some nursing home, away from my family, with no visitors and no reason to live."

"Eventually?" repeated Mom sarcastically.

"I'm serious, Olivia, that would be a fate worse than death for me; you know that."

Mom looked deep into Grandma Helen's eyes and saw a vulnerability people rarely ever see.

"Listen, you may drive me crazy, but I love you too much to ever put you in a place that's going to stifle you and make you unhappy," said Mom. "I would never do something like that to you."

"Really?" she asked. "Because I absolutely hate gardening and have no intention of ever playing Bingo."

"You have my word," said Mom, giving her a hug.

"Thank you, darling," she smiled, hugging her back. "Because I'd hate to have to sue you for breach of contract."

"Oh, my God, are you still holding me to that ridiculous contract you had me sign?" said Mom, rolling her eyes. "It's not even legal and would never stand up in a court of law, you and I both know that."

"Yes, but you still signed it, my dear," retorted Grandma Helen smugly. "And since you continually pride yourself on never falling back on your word, it may as well be legally binding."

"You got me drunk while watching *Terms of Endearment*, I think most would agree that that was a manipulative move," said Mom. "But you're right, I do always keep my word, so I guess I'm stuck with you."

"Uh, hello?" interrupted Aunt Christine. "Are the three of you planning on joining us sometime today?" She dramatically gestured toward an open book lying on a nearby table. "Christian and I really need your help figuring out the wedding bouquet."

"I'm sure whatever you choose will be lovely, dear," smiled Grandma Helen. "You know I've never been one to care much about flowers."

"Oh, okay," she nodded happily. "Daisies it is, then."

"Over my dead body!" yelled Grandma Helen, immediately casting Mom aside. "Those are dreadful flowers used by simpletons, Christine. You may as well be walking down the aisle with grass clippings tied in a string of twine."

One hour later, fifteen minutes of which had been spent assuring Grandma Helen that daisies would not be making an appearance in the wedding, we were saying goodbye to Christian and discussing the plans for the wine tasting this coming Friday.

"Oh, I just love it when my brides have wine tastings!" boasted Christian. "Are we still planning on meeting at Dot's?"

"Yes, we are," answered Mom. "I spoke with Rob last Saturday, and he has eight different wines he wants us to try. We decided that 1:00 would probably be the best time to get started since he's having another tasting later that afternoon."

"Excellent!" he said, clapping his hands excitedly. "And, how many are planning on joining us?"

"Uh, let's see," said Aunt Christine. "Me, Ollie, Addie, Mom, and I believe Nancy's planning on joining us as well, so with you, that makes six."

"Ugh, I still cannot believe you extended an invitation to that woman," sneered Grandma Helen. "She's going to siphon the fun right out of everything."

"I'm sorry, who's Nancy?" asked Christian. "Have I met her yet?"

"Oh, believe me, you'd know if you met her, dear," answered Grandma Helen. "She's an absolute wretch of a woman, who is not only presumptuous, churlish, and ungracious, but also impertinent, tacky, and—"

"She's Brian's mother," interrupted Aunt Christine, looking irritably over at Grandma Helen. "And she's nowhere near as awful as you're making her out to be, so just stop, okay?"

"And since she's offering to pay for all the wine and liquor for the wedding," interjected Mom, "We felt an invitation would be the polite thing to do."

"By all means, invite the spawn of Satan to the wine tasting," shrugged Grandma Helen nonchalantly. "Let's just pray we're able to keep our souls intact once it's over."

"Well, this sounds like it's going to be fun," smirked Christian mischievously. "Just be sure to let me know if I need to bring my crucifix with me. I'm really not in the mood to be possessed."

He gave us each a hug and then sauntered leisurely out the front door.

"Oh, I absolutely adore that man!" beamed Grandma Helen, watching him leave. "And he has such exceptional taste. Did you see the way he effortlessly brought all of those beautiful fall colors together? I'm telling you, Christine, this wedding is going to be gorgeous!"

"The colors really are stunning, aren't they?" said Aunt Christine.

"They're beyond beautiful," said Mom. "This is going to be the perfect fall—"

She cut herself off as her phone began to ring.

"Hold on just one second, Beau's Facetiming me." She swiped to answer the call. "Hello honey, is everything alright?"

"Mom, I can't get this packet of beef jerky open," he said, by way of greeting. "I've been trying for five minutes and it just won't budge."

"You can't possibly be serious right now," she said, stopping midway out the door.

"What? It's not opening, see?" He held up the packet of beef jerky in order to prove his point. "I tore it open where it says to, but it's still sealed."

"Son, please don't tell me you're letting a package of beef jerky beat you," she sighed.

"I'm telling you, Mom, they do this stuff on purpose," he answered emphatically. "I think it's a conspiracy. You know, like when you have to press one for English? I mean, why do we have to push anything? Did America move or something?"

"Beau, honey, I can't do this right now," said Mom. "We're about to leave the florist."

"Okay, fine," he conceded. "But I want to go on record as saying that holding someone's beef jerky hostage is not cool!"

"Dude, you're still struggling with that?" came Ezra's voice in the background. "Just use scissors."

"Oh, that's right, we have scissors!" said Beau. "Why didn't I think of that?"

"Because you're an idiot," answered Ezra.

"Shut up, Ezra!" he spat. "You're such a—"

And with that, the call ended.

Chapter Thirteen

The following evening, Mom and I were in the process of making dinner when her cell phone began to ring.

"Addie, honey, could you please see who's calling?" asked Mom, her hands covered in a teriyaki meatball mixture. "I literally just stuck my hands in all of this."

"It's Ezra," I said, looking at the caller ID. I laid the phone on the counter where she was working and swiped to answer. Here, I'll put it on speaker."

"Hello?" she called out loudly. "I'm sorry, honey, but I've just started to mix up the meatballs for dinner. Can you hear me alright?"

"Yeah, I can hear you," he said.

"Okay, good." She blew a loose strand of hair from her face. "Is everything alright?"

"Well, everything was going great until my belt broke," he huffed. "Now my pants feel like they're going to fall off."

"Your pants aren't going to fall off, Ezra," she said, kneading the mixture in the bowl. "Just come home and get a different belt, and all will be fine."

"I can't," he said. "I don't have another one."

"Yes, you do," she countered. "There are four or five hanging in your closet right now; I've seen them."

"Uh, those are from when I was twelve, Mom," he scoffed. "They obviously no longer fit."

"Then why are they still hanging in your closet?" said Mom, her voice rising an octave.

"I don't know, I guess I just got used to seeing them in there," he answered. "It's not like I pay a lot of attention to what's in there."

"That's because the majority of your clothes carpet your floor," she grumbled. "You know what, never mind. Just swing by Walmart and grab one. You can buy a nicer one later."

"Ugh, fine," he sighed. "But I hope you know that none of this would have happened had you just taken a keener interest in my wardrobe accessories."

"Goodbye, Ezra," she said, nodding at me to disconnect the call.

I ended the call and then stirred a few cups of water into a pot of rice. "Mom, do you honestly think that man/child's ever going to be able to live life on his own?"

"Someday, yes," answered Mom. "I mean, he is part-owner of a successful landscaping company and will eventually be graduating from college next year, so it could be a lot worse. At least that's what I keep telling myself."

Twenty minutes later, after we had just finished snapping the ends off a pound of green beans, Mom's phone rang again.

"Hello?" answered Mom.

"Mom, I had no idea Walmart carried so many cool Lego sets," said Ezra. "I have got to get one."

"Ezra, you're 21 years old; you don't need a Lego set," countered Mom. "Besides, you're there to get a new work belt, so just grab one and come on home."

"Okay, fine," he said dejectedly. "But I'm totally putting one of these on my Christmas list!"

"I'm sure Santa will be thrilled to bring one for you, honey," she snarked. "Just make sure you stay on the nice list. Santa doesn't bring Legos to naughty boys and girls."

Ten minutes later, Mom's phone rang again.

"Yes, Ezra," answered Mom, looking at the caller ID. "What is it this time?"

"Oh my God, Mom, they have the *Doctor Who* set with doctors nine through twelve," he said excitedly. "I have to have this!"

"I said no Legos, Ezra," said Mom. "You're there to look for a belt, remember?"

"It's not a Lego set; it's a DVD set," he clarified. "Think of it, Mom, 112 hours of uninterrupted *Doctor Who* episodes. It's everything I could possibly want."

"I thought you wanted Legos," she drawled sarcastically.

"Nah, I'm over that now," he said.

"How much is it?" she asked.

"That's the thing— it's only $50," he exclaimed. "It's practically a steal!"

"I thought you intended to buy that new video game that comes out next week," I said. "Do you really think spending $50 on a DVD now is wise?"

"It's *Doctor* Who," he responded snobbishly. "Of course it's wise."

"Okay, fine, do what you want," said Mom. "I have a dinner to prepare. But please, Ezra, just go to the belt section and buy a belt."

"Yes, ma'am," he answered obediently.

"Mmm, something smells good," said Dad, walking into the kitchen. "What are you making for dinner?"

"Teriyaki meatballs, rice, and green beans," said Mom, ending the call. "We should be ready to eat in about fifteen minutes."

"Okay, no worries," he smiled. "Just let me know if you need any help."

Ten minutes later, just as we were about to serve dinner, Mom's phone rang once again.

"What is it now, Ezra?" she answered, as calmly as she could.

"Okay, so I'm in the belt section," he said. "But there's this plastic thing on every belt that makes it impossible for me to try on. How am I supposed to even know if it fits?"

"I don't know, maybe the tag on the belt telling you the actual size?" she snarked. "You know, S for small, M for medium, and so on…"

"Uh, yeah, none of these belts have that, Mom," he shot back. "I'm at Walmart, remember?"

"Oh, for the love of God, Ezra, just put the belt around your waist and see if the holes align with the buckle," she said irritably. "It's not rocket science!"

"Well, you don't have to get all snippy about it," he snapped. "I just didn't want to get the wrong size, that's all."

"I'm sorry, but it shouldn't take three phone calls to buy a belt, Ezra," said Mom, her tone softening. "I tell you what, why don't you try one on while I'm on the phone and then let me know if it fits."

"Actually, I think this one'll fit, but I'll go ahead and double-check anyway." After a momentary pause, he came back on the line. "Yep, this one fits perfectly. Thanks, Mom!"

"You're welcome, honey," she said, pulling dishes out of the cabinet. "Oh, by the way, I meant to ask, what is that whirring sound I keep hearing? Is your phone acting up?"

"Oh, no, it's not my phone," he said. "I think it's coming from the scooter."

"What scooter?" asked Mom.

"The store scooter," he answered jovially. "Have you ever ridden one of these things? They are so cool!"

"Oh, my God, Ezra, those are for disabled people!" yelled Mom into the phone. "Go and return that thing right now!"

"Geez, Mom, calm down," he said. "There were like 30 of them sitting there, and no one was using them, so it's really not that big of a deal. Besides, my pants felt like they were going to fall down, and since I didn't feel like giving everyone a peep show, it only made sense to take one."

The continual whirring sound of the scooter could be heard in the background as Mom stood in the kitchen, pinching the bridge of her nose in frustration.

"Okay, I put the scooter back with the other 29 that haven't moved," said Ezra, "Are you happy now?"

"I am, yes," she said. "Thank you. Now, go ahead and pay for everything, and I'll be sure to make you a plate for dinner. That way, you can heat it up when you get here."

"Okay, I'll be home soon," he said. "I love you."

"I love you too," she said.

Ending the call, Mom blew out a long breath and immediately grabbed a glass and the bottle of Cabernet sitting on the counter.

"Tell me, Addie, do you think it's still considered neglect and abuse if I choose to lock myself in a closet?"

***

Later that evening, Mom and Dad were sitting in the living room while Beau, who is the slowest person on Earth when it comes to doing something he doesn't want to do, begrudgingly helped me finish cleaning up the kitchen.

"How is it that I've been able to clean up all the dishes, the stove, the countertops, and the kitchen table in the same amount of time it's taken you to put away the teriyaki sauce and take out the trash?" I asked. "Seriously, Beau, you can't possibly be that indolent."

"Okay, first of all, I don't even know what that means," he retorted sourly. "And secondly, the slower I go, the less I usually end up doing, so you really only have yourself to blame. I mean, I'm perfectly happy taking all night to do this, but you're the one who wants to get it done quickly, so…"

"You're an incorrigible miscreant," I sneered.

"Yeah, well, I've been called worse," he shrugged.

As we walked into the living room to join Mom and Dad, Beau stopped short just outside of the sitting area and smiled mischievously. "Uh oh, I think I feel a small airplane in the hangar."

"Beau, don't," warned Mom.

"It's too late, Mom; it already flew out," he grinned. "Fly free, my friend!"

"Oh, my God, you are so gross!" I yelled, covering my mouth. "I think I'm actually going to be sick."

"Okay, enough with the theatrics, Addie," chided Mom. "Beau, you have got to stop…" She paused and then immediately covered her nose with her hand. "Oh, dear God, that is absolutely abhorrent!"

"Yeah, I think it's kind of clinging to me," he said, wafting his hand behind him. "I don't think it's going anywhere anytime soon."

"My God, it's like napalm!" exclaimed Dad, waving his magazine to clear the air. "At least have the decency to walk out of the room, Son. I think you've singed my nose hairs."

"Aww, I love you too, Dad," he smiled. "Okay, well, I'm going to head over to Tyler's for a while. I'll be back later."

"Ugh, don't come back if you're planning on doing more of that," I said, still plugging my nose. "We'll have to call in Hazmat."

Dad watched Beau walk out the back door and then immediately turned his attention back to Mom and me. "I'm telling you, if they could figure out a way to bottle that, we wouldn't need nuclear weapons."

"I know, right?" said Mom, scrunching up her nose. "I mean, it's still lingering."

Once the putrid stench had dissipated and the air was finally breathable again, Mom's phone began to ring. Looking at the display, she could see that it was Grandma Helen calling.

"Hi, Mom, what's up?" she said.

"Darling, what's the name of that little wine place we're going to tomorrow?" asked Grandma Helen.

"Dot's Fine Wine and Craft, why?"

"Oh, I'm just texting some of the girls about it," she said. "If I find it charming enough, we may think about planning a girl's day up there. We simply adore the Bistro but thought it might be fun to change it up from time to time. Anyway, I really need to get back to them. TTFN!"

"Ugh, why did I have to recommend using Dot's for the wedding?" Mom moaned despairingly. "Now, we're not going to have any place that's just ours. This sucks."

Two years ago, Mom and Dad happened upon a fun little wine shop in the heart of downtown Ball Ground, a quaint small town that is located about 15 minutes north of Canton. After spending an afternoon sipping and learning about various wines from around the world, they were immediately smitten and eagerly made plans to come back as often as possible. So now, anytime they have a chance to sneak away together, that is where they go. It was their little secret, their oasis— A place where they could sip wine and just be together. Or at least, that's what it was until Mom decided to tell Aunt Christine about it a little over a month ago.

"Yeah, Mom, why did you tell her about that place?" I asked. "You usually don't like to share information like that."

"Because 36 days ago, your mother drank entirely too much Pinot and drunkenly told Rob and Mindy that she thought they would be the perfect wine supplier for your aunt's wedding," said Dad. "Then two days later, after we both decided that wasn't a good idea, she drank too much Chardonnay and decided to flaunt our favorite private haunt to her sister, who, in turn, decided to share that same information with your grandmother. Isn't that right, honey?"

"Ugh, yes," she muttered quietly. "I am solely to blame."

"And that, my darling daughter," said Dad, opening his magazine, "is why your mother and I can't have nice things.

CHAPTER FOURTEEN

Dot's Fine Wine and Craft is owned by Rob and Mindy Harrison, a married couple, who, not so long ago, decided to trade in the craziness of Midtown Atlanta for the slower paced, more hometown feel of North Georgia. After years of owning and operating a slew of successful restaurants, the two decided to open up a small wine store in the heart of Ball Ground, where everyone, from the savviest of drinkers to those just starting out could enjoy fine wine and beer from all around the world. With Rob being a top-level sommelier and Mindy an experienced cicerone, they have managed to create a successful wine boutique that happily caters to all types of oenophiles, both young and old.

As I walked into Dot's that afternoon, I immediately understood why my parents loved it so much. It was the kind of place that made you feel right at home. It was warm, inviting, and hummed with the continual chatter of light-hearted conversation and easygoing banter. Its dusky blue shelves, filled with wines from around the world, climbed vertically up exposed brick walls, creating a vast display of varietals that would cause any wine enthusiast to stop and take notice. Cozy nooks furnished with plush armchairs in warm shades of tangerine and chestnut were scattered around the store, while the soft sound of Peter Gabriel's "*Solsbury Hill*" could be heard quietly playing in the background.

This was more than just a wine store. It was a place to pause, to sip, and to savor. It was the kind of space where strangers became friends over a shared bottle of wine, and time, like the wine, just seemed to flow a little bit slower.

"Hey, Olivia," said a man in a pink shirt behind the counter. "Just give me a few minutes and I'll be right with you."

"Take your time, Rob," smiled Mom, waving a greeting. "We're in no hurry."

"My God, he looks exactly like Stanley Tucci!" exclaimed Grandma Helen.

"You say that about every bald man with glasses you see, Mother," said Aunt Christine.

Seeing Christian trying to make sense of the comparison, Mom leaned in and said, "We've been watching a lot of *Tucci in Italy* lately, so she's become a bit obsessed with him."

"Oh, my God, I love that show!" beamed Christian excitedly. "I tell you, that man looks simply dashing in a scarf and sunglasses." He put his hand over his chest and laughed. "You know, normally I'd be offended by seeing what that man is willing to eat, but he can make even a lampredotto sandwich sound appetizing, which is something I'd never thought I'd say."

"What's a lampredotto sandwich?" I asked.

"It's a Florentine street food made from the fourth stomach of a cow," he answered knowledgeably. "Apparently, you're supposed to dip it in au jus, just like you would a French dip."

"Ew, I'm sorry I asked," I shuddered, feeling my stomach roil at the thought. I turned and looked at Mom. "And you're telling me grandma actually watches this show?"

"Oh, I absolutely love it, dear!" exclaimed Grandma Helen. "I've learned so much about Italy from watching him." She tucked her arm through mine and looked up at me. "You know, dear, Stanley Tucci is not just a phenomenal entertainer; he's also an avid scholar and accomplished culinarian. And, yes, if I'm being honest, he does tend to consume a variety of questionable foods from time-to-time, but I feel that only adds to his eccentricity and peculiarity, which, at least for me, has always been a part of his allure."

"Accomplished culinarian?" asked Aunt Christine. "Are you sure about that?"

"The man is constantly cooking and sharing recipes on his Instagram, Christine," she replied. "So, yes, he's an accomplished culinarian."

"Like I said, obsessed," muttered Mom, rolling her eyes.

"Hey there," smiled Rob, walking over to us. "I'm so sorry to keep you waiting, but unfortunately, I'm on my own until Mindy gets here."

He looked down at his watch. "She should be here any minute, so if you'd like to go ahead and take a seat back in the tasting room, I'll be with you as soon as she gets here."

"Yes, of course," said Mom. "Take your time. We're still waiting for one more person, anyway."

"Ugh, can't we just lock her out?" grumbled Grandma Helen.

"Don't start, Mother," warned Aunt Christine. "You promised you'd behave, remember?"

"Oh, come now, behaving is so overrated," snickered Christian. "It's always so much more fun not to, don't you think, Helen?"

"I most certainly do, my dear!" she declared boldly.

"Alright, that's it," said Mom, stepping in between them. "The two of you are not allowed to sit together during the tasting. You'll only feed off each other and make things worse."

"No worries, Helen, we'll just use hand signals," whispered Christian with a wink.

The tasting room was a quiet and secluded area toward the back of the store. Red exposed brick walls, their weathered surface lending an aged look, were adorned with three large black and white photos of the most adorable-looking Jack Russell Terrier. At the room's center stood a long, rectangular, wooden table resting atop a once colorful Persian rug whose edges had now become frayed with age and use. Three white metal chairs flanked both sides of the table, each perched in front of a large place setting holding two tasting boards and eight small glasses. At the head of the table sat three bottles of red and white wine, while two tall ice buckets, each holding a single bottle of sparkling wine, stood at either corner.

"Ooh, I love anything sparkling!" exclaimed Grandma Helen, reaching for one of the bottles. "Let's see, is it Prosecco or Champagne?"

"Don't touch anything," hissed Mom, slapping her hand away. "We need to wait for Rob."

"Well, it's not my fault that his wife isn't here on time," she retorted sourly. "You'd think he would at least let us have a drink while we wait."

"Oh, my God, this dog is so cute!" I smiled, pointing at one of the pictures. "Does he belong to Rob and Mindy?"

"Yes, that's Stanley," said Mom. "And before you ask, Mother, no, they did not name him after Stanley Tucci." She sidled up next to me and looked up at the picture. "He's definitely adorable, that's for sure, but whatever you do, don't pet him. He doesn't like strangers and will literally bite your finger off if you get too close."

"But look at that face," cooed Christian. "He certainly doesn't look menacing."

"Trust me, many people have overestimated their ability to tame Stanley," said Mom. "There are signs all around the front counter warning people not to touch him, but they never listen. Inevitably, there's always some unfortunate soul who thinks they're the drunk dog whisperer and winds up paying the price."

"Then why on earth would they ever bring him into this store?" asked Grandma Helen.

"It's their store, Mother, they can do whatever they want," said Mom. "Stanley's had a tough life. He's a rescue, and both Rob and Mindy want to make him happy. He hates being away from them, so they built him a little nook behind the counter. If someone's stupid enough not to heed the multiple warnings, then they deserve what they get."

"Hello, everyone," said Nancy, walking into the room. "I apologize for being late." She set down a large brown paper bag on the table. "It's nice to see that you haven't started without me."

"Well, it certainly wasn't for lack of trying," muttered Grandma Helen.

"I was on my way over here when I saw these two little German ladies dressed in Dirndls grilling sausages next door," she explained. "Tom and I absolutely love German food, so I took a quick peek inside and thought I'd buy a few things to add to our tasting." She slowly began pulling out items wrapped in white butcher paper. "Let's see, I've got smoked liverwurst pate with crackers, some cheddar and jalapeno leberkäse, olive leberkäse, and in a few minutes, they'll be bringing over a smattering of smoked sausages they offered to throw on the grill for me."

"That was so sweet of you, Nancy, thank you," smiled Aunt Christine.

"German food at a wine tasting?" snickered Grandma Helen. "How uncouth."

"Uh, Nancy, I don't believe you've met Christian, my wedding coordinator," said Aunt Christine, diverting the conversation. "He's been an absolute Godsend in helping me plan all of this."

"Hello, Christian," she smiled primly, folding the brown paper bag in her hand. "It's good to meet you."

"It's nice to meet you, too," he said, holding out his hand. Realizing she had absolutely no intention of shaking it, he briefly glanced over at Grandma Helen and said, "I've heard so much about you."

"Yes, I'm sure you have," answered Nancy, looking over her shoulder at Grandma Helen. "Although I would encourage you not to believe everything you hear."

"Nancy, darling!" exclaimed Grandma Helen, walking over to her. "It's so wonderful of you to join us today." She then made it a point to look over at Aunt Christine. "Tell me, dear, are we supposed to be having a beer tasting today as well?"

"No, only wine, why?" she asked.

"Well, I hate to point out the obvious," said Grandma Helen sardonically. "But wine really pairs better with a nice charcuterie, don't you think?" She glanced down at the table and curled her lip slightly. "Now, don't get me wrong, I'm sure German cuisine is absolutely wonderful when paired with the right type of beer, if you like that sort of thing, but I have found that wine really requires a much more refined palate. As such, Olivia and I have arranged for a few charcuterie platters to be delivered specifically for that purpose." She looked over at Mom. "Isn't that right, dear?"

"Uh, yes," smiled Mom uneasily. "Although I can personally vouch that anything from Frankfurt Döner & Meats is absolutely outstanding, so I'm sure it will be a wonderful addition to the charcuterie."

"Actually, Helen," began Nancy. "German cuisine, with its rich and hearty flavors, is known to pair beautifully with all different types of wine, both domestic and international. For example, the bright acidity and elegant balance of a Riesling can often help enhance the savory and salty character found in many Germanic traditional dishes, while the delicate and smooth notes of a Pinot Blanc can often cut through the sharp tanginess of sauerkraut and the golden crunch of a fried schnitzel. Of course, my personal favorite would have to be the light bodied Spätburgunder, which is the German equivalent to a Pinot Noir. It's an absolutely lovely wine that pairs effortlessly with the smoky depth of any type of sausage, or the tender succulence of a slow-roasted pork." She fiddled with one of the tasting boards on the table, making sure to align it perfectly with the others. "So, when you actually take the time to think about it, both wine and food, regardless of nationality, often speak the same language. One that many in the wine world believe is steeped in comfort, tradition, and quiet indulgence."

"Oh wow, that was absolutely amazing!" exclaimed Christian, clapping his hands together. "Bravo!"

"I had no idea that you knew so much about wine," said Aunt Christine. "You're going to be a great help today."

"Oh, it's just something I recently started learning about," dismissed Nancy. "I'm still very much an amateur. In fact, I'm really hoping to learn a good bit more from Rob today."

"Well, Rob loves it when people take an interest in wine," said Mom. "I'm sure he'll be thrilled to answer any questions you may have. He loves sharing his knowledge."

As we all began taking our seats around the table, Nancy watched in amusement as the look of pure vexation washed over Grandma Helen's face. Sauntering over to her, Nancy leaned in closely and whispered. "You're not the only one who knows how to use Google, my friend." She gently laid her hand on Grandma Helen's shoulder, then pulled back to look her in the eyes. "You know, I'm really glad that Tom and Anthony have become friends. They're like a couple of schoolgirls who tell each other everything." She pulled out a chair and slowly lowered herself into it. "I guess male bonding isn't overrated after all."

With her fists clenched at her side, Grandma Helen coolly walked over to the chair between Mom and me and sat down.

"I absolutely abhor that woman," she hissed.

"Calm down, Mom, it's not worth it," said Mom.

"Okay, fine, I'm calm," she breathed out. "But just so you know, your father is a dead man."

Before Mom had a chance to respond, the door to the tasting room swung open.

"Okay, everybody!" exclaimed Rob, rubbing his hands together excitedly. "Let's get ready to taste some wine." Walking over to the table, he immediately noticed the food and yelled out, "Yes! Leberkäse … my favorite. It works perfectly with the Riesling I've selected for you."

Chapter Fifteen

"Oh, my God, these sausages are to die for!" exclaimed Christian. "And this pate is absolutely incredible." He greedily reached for another link of sausage. "I mean, I can't stop myself from eating it all, it's so good! And you're right, Rob, this Riesling pairs perfectly with both."

He looked across the table to see Grandma Helen staring daggers at him and mouthed apologetically, "I'm sorry, but it does."

"Greg and I always make sure to get something from Frankfurt Döner & Meats whenever we come up here," smiled Mom. "We usually like to share the Döner sandwich, which, if you haven't had it, is the best sandwich I've ever had." She cut herself a piece of leberkäse and placed it on top of a cracker. "In fact, I think they were even featured in the local news for that very thing a few weeks ago, right, Rob?"

"They were, yes," nodded Rob. "And now people from all over the state of Georgia are coming up to Ball Ground to try what has now been dubbed, 'The Life-Changing Sandwich.'"

"Life changing?" grumbled Grandma Helen. "I highly doubt that."

"No, seriously, it's amazing," said Rob. "You really must try one, or at least take one home while you're here."

"I'm really not much of a sandwich person, dear," replied Grandma Helen, curling her lip. "Unless, of course, it's a Monte Cristo. I find that I can always make an exception for that."

"You mean deep-fried French toast layered high with processed meat, cheese, and sugar," drawled Mom. "I shudder to think how many calories are in that thing."

"Yes, well, unlike you, I really don't need to worry about such things," smiled Grandma Helen. "I've always been so petite; it's really never been much of a concern for me."

"Listen, I've seen the pictures of you after childbirth, and know that that is a big fat lie," said Mom. "In fact, I believe you were sprawled out on the couch, wearing a muumuu, and eating ice cream in one of them."

"I most certainly was not!" she spat angrily. "I have never sprawled a day in my life, Olivia. You've obviously mistaken me with someone else."

"No, it was you," smiled Mom. "I'm pretty sure I have the picture somewhere. I'll find it."

"Don't you dare!" she hissed quietly. "I mean it, Olivia, don't."

"Okay, fine," said Mom, turning to face her. "But make another rude comment like that again, and I promise you that I'll not only find it, but I'll have it blown up and placed on a billboard over on I-575 for everyone to see."

Before she had a chance to respond, Mom turned back toward the table and smiled angelically. "Nancy, again, thank you so much for bringing in all of this delicious food. It was very kind of you."

"Yes, of course, I was more than happy to." She sneered triumphantly over at Grandma Helen before looking up at Rob timidly. "I just hope I haven't ruined your tasting by bringing all of it in."

"Are you kidding?" said Rob. "These dishes are perfect to pair with all different types of wine. In fact—"

"I'm so sorry, dear," interrupted Grandma Helen, looking at her Apple Watch. "But I have to be somewhere shortly after we finish with all of this. Would it be possible for us to just go ahead and taste the next wine?"

"Oh, yes, of course," smiled Rob. "We only have one left, so it really shouldn't take too long."

Knowing full well that Grandma Helen had nowhere else to be, Aunt Christine, Mom, and I looked oddly at each other before Mom leaned in close to her and whispered, "What exactly are you doing? You don't have anywhere else to be. We set all day aside for this, remember?"

"Yes, dear, I remember," answered Grandma Helen quietly. "But if I have to sit here and watch that woman smirk at me every time someone mentions how fantastic that damn meat parade is that she brought in here, I'm going to scream." She drained the last of the wine in her tasting glass and set it back down. "And these tiny little glasses of wine aren't doing anywhere near enough to help me tolerate her, so that was the best I could do under duress."

"Well, you're going to look like an idiot after we're finished because we were planning on staying for another bottle or two afterward, or don't you remember demanding that of us earlier today?" asked Mom.

"Plans change and get cancelled all the time, Olivia," she shrugged dismissively. "I'll simply say that my friend had some sort of emergency and needed to reschedule. No one will even know, unless, of course, you decide to betray me like your father did."

"Yeah, what's that even about, anyway?" asked Mom.

"I really don't want to talk about it right now, dear; the wound is still fresh." She picked up another tasting glass and drained the last of it. "Just know that he will definitely be getting his comeuppance for what he did, the rat bastard."

"Okay, so this wine, right here, is the Juan Gil Blue Label from Jumilla, Spain," said Rob, lifting the last bottle of red. "It is a truly remarkable wine that delivers exceptional taste without breaking the bank. It's crafted primarily from old vine Monastrell but is also supported by a blend of Cabernet and Syrah that help lend additional depth and structure. The color is absolutely brilliant, and the taste is undeniably delicious."

Slowly lifting the glass to his nose, he asked, "So, tell me, what is it that you smell, exactly?"

"Um, I'd say that it smells like some sort of dark fruit, and maybe a little bit of coffee," said Nancy, inhaling deeply. "I think I'm also getting a hint of spice."

"Okay, yes, very good," nodded Rob encouragingly. "Anyone else?"

"Uh, and maybe a bit of black currant?" asked Christian dubiously.

"Okay, that's certainly a possibility," said Rob. He looked around the room, settling his eyes on Grandma Helen. "And what about you, Helen? What exactly do you smell?"

"Honestly, I just smell red wine," she answered plainly.

He laughed at what he thought was a joke and then said, "No, seriously, I'm really curious as to what it is you smell." He swirled the wine in his glass and held it back up to his nose. "Does it remind you of anything specific? Perhaps a certain fruit or spice?"

"Not really, no," she shook her head.

"Surely, there's something that comes to mind," he pressed. "Is it peppery? Is it fruity? Is it earthy? There are so many possibilities whenever it comes to wine."

"I tell you what, dear," said Grandma Helen. "Why don't you just tell me what it is that you smell, and then I'll let you know if I smell that too."

"Be nice, Mother," warned Mom quietly.

"Okay, well, I would have to say that this wine definitely unveils a wonderful bouquet of ripe blackberries, cassis, and roasted coffee," answered Rob. "But there is also a layer of sweet spice, cocoa, and cedar to it that is somewhat faint, but still present." He lifted his glass in recognition to Nancy and Christian. "So, it would seem that the two of you were both correct. Bravo!"

"Well, that's only because you've been such a wonderful teacher, Rob," gushed Nancy. "I just can't believe how much I'm learning in such a short time."

"Ugh, could she be any more obnoxious?" hissed Grandma Helen. "She's such a sycophant."

"You're just mad because she's beating you at this," snickered Mom.

"Well, she wouldn't be if I were actually trying," she mumbled.

"Okay, so now I want everyone to take a small sip and then slowly let it envelope your tongue," said Rob. "Swish it around and then let it rest in your mouth for a few seconds. I think you're going to find that the flavor profile is both sumptuous and full-bodied, with velvety tannins that carry a slight wave of dark fruit and mocha." He lifted his glass and took a sip. "One of the great things about this particular wine is that it showcases the sun-drenched, limestone-rich soils that are found in southeastern Spain. That's what gives it its savory mineral edge. So, despite the intensity, it remains beautifully balanced and lifted, which is a testament to the warm Mediterranean terroir that surrounds it."

"I'm so sorry to interrupt you, Rob, but what exactly does terroir mean?" asked Nancy. "I can't say I'm familiar with that term."

"Oh, dear God, can she possibly get her head any further up his ass?" sneered Grandma Helen. "It's absolutely pathetic."

"She wants to learn, Mother," said Mom. "Which is more than I can say for you."

"Terroir is the French term for the natural environment in which a particular wine is produced," said Rob. "So, factors like soil, topography, and climate all come into play whenever we look at what affects a particular grape's phenotype."

"Is that so?" said Nancy, completely entranced. "I had no idea so much went into the winemaking process. It's almost as if it's both a science and an art."

"I couldn't agree more, Nancy," smiled Rob warmly. "You see, wine is a storyteller. It has a thousand different voices, and each bottle carries its own distinct temperament. It's steeped in human history and shaped by its origins and upbringing. So, in many ways, wine has its own story to tell, just like every person does. It's distinctive and individualistic, just like we are."

"What a lovely analogy, Rob," smiled Grandma Helen, suddenly taking interest in the conversation. "So, tell me, in addition to the flavor profile, which is simply divine, by the way, and the fact that its intensity is undoubtedly related to its unique Mediterranean terroir, what else can you tell us about this wine?"

"Okay, you really need to stop using words you know nothing about," whispered Mom, leaning in close. "Not three minutes ago, you couldn't care less about anything other than getting a buzz, and now you suddenly understand flavor profile?"

"I'm going to show that woman that I can play her game just as well as she can," said Grandma Helen. "Except I'm not going to look like an ass while doing it."

"I think it's a little too late for that," snarked Mom.

Rob gave Grandma Helen a dubious look before answering her question. "Uh, well, other than what's already been said, I'd say that this is a wine with a lot of confidence and character. That it can hold its own against many of the more well-known wines from the Bordeaux and Napa regions, and um, that it is a perfect wine to serve for any occasion."

"Well, I definitely think that this would be a perfect addition to the wine we've already chosen," said Christian, draining his glass. "What do you think, Christine?"

"It's phenomenal," she said, nodding her head in agreement. "I definitely think this should be our red."

"Excellent!" boasted Rob. "I'll go ahead and order the Juan Gil in addition to the Trimbach Riesling and Monteros Cava Brut you decided on earlier." He reached down to pick up a few empty glasses. "I think you made great choices, Christine. These wines will complement your menu perfectly."

"I think so too," she smiled. "Thank you."

Making it a point to look down at her phone with mock disappointment, Grandma Helen acted like she was reading a text.

"Ugh, I can't believe this," she groaned. "Joan just cancelled on me."

"Oh, dear God, please don't," whispered Mom, closing her eyes in embarrassment.

"Apparently, her daughter had an emergency come up and now has to babysit her grandkids," said Grandma Helen, disappointedly. "Oh, that poor thing. She was so looking forward to tonight."

"Oh, was she now?" drawled Aunt Christine sarcastically. "That's funny, because you never made any mention of—"

"So now I guess we're no longer in any rush to leave!" she exclaimed, cutting off Aunt Christine. Picking up her purse, she walked over to the head of the table. "Thank you so much for taking the time to walk us through all of this delicious wine, Rob. Do you think you could be a dear, and maybe recommend a few wines that we might be able to enjoy while we stay here for a little while?"

"Yes, of course, I'd be happy to," he smiled. "What are you in the mood for?"

Linking her arm with his, she beamed up at him. "Well, considering you're the expert, I'm going to leave that decision up to you."

We settled on a bold Argentinian Malbec, and had just finished watching Rob pour the wine, when Nancy and Christian walked over to us.

"Christian, darling," cooed Grandma Helen. "Please go and get yourself a glass and join us. This wine is outstanding."

"I wish I could, but I have dinner plans with a friend of mine," he said. "Perhaps a raincheck?"

"Of course, dear," she smiled. "We'll be sure to plan something soon."

"Nancy, would you like to join us?" asked Aunt Christine, ignoring Grandma Helen's angry glare.

"No, thank you," she answered, returning Grandma Helen's glare. "I believe I've had more than my fill."

"Well, maybe another time, then," said Aunt Christine.

"Here, Nancy, let me take those for you," offered Christian, taking the bags of leftovers from her arms. "I'll help you get them in the car."

"Thank you, Christian," she said, handing them to him. "I'd appreciate that."

"So, now that everything's set for the wedding, I guess I won't be seeing all of you for a few months," said Christian.

"No, I guess you won't," answered Aunt Christine sadly.

"I'll plan on reaching out a few weeks before the wedding, but if you need anything between now and then, please don't hesitate to call," he smiled. "Day or night, it doesn't matter."

"Thank you," said Aunt Christine.

"Alright, Nancy," he gestured grandly toward the door. "Lead the way."

As we watched the two of them walk out the door and over to Nancy's car, Grandma Helen dramatically rolled her eyes. "I can't believe he's helping her."

"He's a gentleman," said Mom. "I'm sure he would do the same for you."

"Of course he would," she answered pompously. "But he's mine. I saw him first."

"He's not a toy, Mother, he's a grown man," said Mom. "You can't lay claim to him."

"Yes, I understand that, dear," she said. "But he's so shiny and bright. If he allows her to get her hooks in him, he'll become dull and boring, and I won't be able to laugh with him anymore."

"Okay, I honestly don't know what any of that is about; nor do I care," said Mom dismissively. "What I do care about, however, is why you're so angry with Dad."

Grandma Helen took in a deep breath and solemnly took a sip of her wine.

"He betrayed me," she sighed.

"What?" we asked in confusion.

"He betrayed me," she reiterated. "He told that deplorable woman's husband all about my Googling those famous authors." She reached for the wine bottle and poured herself another glass. "So, she, in turn, decided to Google all she could about wine, so she could spout off like she's some sort of amateur sommelier, the bitch."

"So, she basically beat you at your own game," said Mom pointedly.

"She did not beat me, Olivia," she spat. "If anything, she copied my brilliant strategy and then used it against me." She crossed her arms in irritation. "But, of course, none of that would have even happened had your father just kept his mouth shut."

"Look, I understand that you're angry, but you don't have any proof that Dad deliberately betrayed you," said Aunt Christine. "Maybe he made a mistake, and it just slipped out."

"Chrissy makes a good point," said Mom.

"Did you tell him not to say anything?" I asked.

"I shouldn't have to!" she answered bitterly. "He's my husband and should know to keep certain things to himself."

"Like when you deliberately arm yourself with knowledge you normally would have no use for except whenever it helps you belittle someone else?" asked Mom, raising her brow. "That kind of thing?"

"Yes, exactly," agreed Grandma Helen testily.

"I know for a fact that Grandpa would never deliberately try to hurt you," I said. "He's not that kind of person. I'm sure there's a good reason he said something."

"Yes, well, whatever that reason is, it's not good enough," she combated. "He made me look like a fool, and in front of that self-righteous, sanctimonious, killjoy of a woman, no less."

"She's not that bad, Mom," said Aunt Christine.

"You know, you may want to try showing Nancy and Dad a little grace," said Mom. "You just might find that it'll make things a little bit easier on you and everyone else."

"Ugh, fine," sighed Grandma Helen. "I'll be gracious and give your father a chance to explain himself, but I have absolutely no interest in ever trying to make nice with that incorrigible woman. You should have heard her today. She was so smug and priggish. I literally just wanted to slap her."

"Yes, well, let's not do that," said Mom, signaling for Rob. "Instead, I say we have another bottle of wine and maybe just calm down a bit. How does that sound?"

"That sounds perfect, darling," smiled Grandma Helen, draining the last of her wine. "However, the minute this wedding is over, the gloves are coming off, and I fully intend to make her suffer."

Chapter Sixteen

It turns out that there was a reason that Grandpa Anthony exposed Grandma Helen's "brilliant" Google strategy to Tim, although I'm not so sure it was a good one. Apparently, he and Tim had a few too many bourbons one night and decided to make a friendly wager on whose wife was the most eccentric. Having absolutely no understanding of the depths of Grandma Helen's unconventionality, Tim found out the hard way that Nancy's peculiarities were mere child's play when compared to Grandma Helen's. So by the end of that night, secrets were shared, bets were lost, and Tim was cleaned out of $500.

Needless to say, Grandpa Anthony received absolutely no grace from Grandma Helen and ended up in the doghouse for quite some time. It's been almost three months now, and she's only recently stopped giving him the cold shoulder.

As for the wedding, we're now less than a week away, and things are really starting to gain momentum. With the bridal luncheon tomorrow and the rehearsal dinner on Friday everyone is really getting into the spirit. Well, everyone except Mom and Aunt Christine, that is. They made the unfortunate mistake of getting inebriated at Aunt Christine's impromptu bachelorette party last night and are currently doing their best to recuperate from a long night of drunken revelry.

"Oh, my God, why did you let me drink so much last night?" moaned Mom. "My body doesn't recover like it used to."

"And mine does?" said Aunt Christine, holding a cold compress to her forehead. "This is no picnic for me either, you know."

"Did either of you even contemplate drinking water throughout the night?" I asked, refilling their coffee cups.

"Please tell me that's a rhetorical question," said Ezra, coming downstairs. "You only have to look at them to know the answer." He walked into the kitchen and opened the refrigerator. "Besides, who has time for water when tequila's so readily available?"

"It wasn't tequila," said Mom. "And for the love of God, please stop talking about alcohol. I feel bad enough as it is, I don't need any extra help from you."

"Well, just know that I'm here if you change your mind," he smirked.

"Here, take some ibuprofen," I said, handing them three pills each. "It should help get rid of your headache, at least."

"Bless you, my child," said Mom, gratefully.

"You know, I've been thinking," said Beau, coming into the kitchen.

"Uh-oh, that's both surprising and frightening," snarked Ezra, pouring cereal into a bowl.

"No, I'm serious," he said. "I was watching this show about squirt guns the other day and started to think how a squirt gun filled with canned tuna water could be a fairly devastating weapon. I mean, it's nonlethal, yes, but imagine how putrid and rotten that smell would be? In fact, you could probably even add in some chopped sardines and really—"

"Please stop talking," interrupted Aunt Christine, holding her hand up. "I don't think I can handle listening to the rest of that sentence."

"But…" he continued.

"Nope," she shook her head, looking a little green. "I'm on the verge of throwing up as it is, and I really don't feel like having to make a run for the toilet right now."

"Well, maybe you should rethink some of the choices that got you into that predicament in the first place," countered Beau. "You know, like saying 'no, thank you,' when the bartender offers you another drink." He opened and closed a few of the kitchen cabinets and then asked, "Hey Mom, do we have one of those small scales that drug dealers use?"

"I'm sorry, what?" asked Mom, slowly rubbing her temples.

"A drug dealer scale," he reiterated. "Do we have one?"

"I think he means a digital food scale," I said, rolling my eyes.

"Yeah, I guess that could work too," he shrugged.

"What do you need a scale for?" asked Ezra.

"I need to weigh some candy," he said. "Tyler and I pulled our money together and bought a big bag of sour gummies at the new candy store downtown. I just want to double-check and make sure he weighed my half correctly," answered Beau.

"Were you not paying attention when you were weighing the candy when you bought it?" I asked.

"I wasn't there. He stopped in with his dad." he said, opening another cabinet door. "I know he's my best friend and all, but when it comes to candy, he really can't be trusted. He tends to be a bit of a glutton, if you know what I mean."

"You mean like you?" drawled Ezra.

"Shut up, jerk!" yelled Beau.

"I believe there's a small scale outside on Dad's workbench," interjected Mom, before the argument could escalate. "Just be sure to return it when you're done."

"Yes, ma'am," he nodded.

Mom slowly sipped her coffee and looked up at Ezra. "Hey, don't forget, you and Beau are supposed to be helping Nana set up for tomorrow's bridal luncheon."

"Yeah, I know," he said. "Nana already called to remind me."

"God, I really hope I feel better by tomorrow," groaned Aunt Christine. "I don't want to look like death warmed over when I see everyone."

"You have over 24 hours to recover," said Mom. "I'm fairly certain you'll be back amongst the land of the living by then."

"Found it!" exclaimed Beau jubilantly, walking back in from the garage.

"Found what?" asked Dad, coming into the kitchen.

"The drug dealer scale you have out in the garage," he said, lifting it up. "I found it."

"That is not a drug dealer scale, son," said Dad, pouring coffee into a mug. "I use it to weigh my bullets when I'm reloading."

"Well, drug dealers might just be using it for that too," he quipped. "You don't know, maybe it's a multifunctional tool for them."

"You know what, never mind," said Dad. "Just be sure to put it back where you found it, okay?"

"Okay, I will," nodded Beau, before turning to lean on the counter in front of Mom and Aunt Christine. "Hey, Mom, why is there a gigantic, pink and yellow, flower piñata hanging up in the corner of the garage?"

"Oh, I'm keeping it for Mary Lou from across the street," answered Mom. "Her daughter's turning six this weekend and I'm helping her hide it until they have the party on Saturday."

"You know, I bet if they filled that pinata up with ketchup, it would look like a blood bath raining down after the first good strike," said Beau excitedly. "Do you think we could do that for my birthday? But instead of a flower, we get a donkey, or some other animal, so that it looks more realistic?"

"No," she answered flatly.

"Oh, come on, Mom, everyone would love it," he grinned. "People would be talking about it for days."

"Which is exactly why the answer is no," she said.

"Well, I bet Tyler's Mom would let him do it," he teased.

"Then, by all means, pass your brilliant idea onto her," said Mom. "I'm more than happy to let her deal with all of those freaked-out parents who will be coming to pick-up their emotionally scarred and ketchup-doused children."

"That's why you tell them to bring extra clothes on the invitation," he beamed. "It's a win-win."

"No," she said firmly.

"Ugh, you're no fun," he huffed, running up the stairs. "I should know better than to ask you for anything when you're hungover."

"You know, it's actually not a bad idea," said Dad, placing a lid on his coffee cup. "At least that way we wouldn't have to worry about hosting another children's birthday party ever again." He kissed Mom on the cheek and then added, "Although we could probably just invite your mother over and have a similar outcome."

"I think I'd prefer the ketchup-filled piñata," deadpanned Mom.

Dad looked over at Aunt Christine and winked. "So, did you tell Brian about your sexy hunk of a bartender?"

"Oh, my God, you told him?" she gasped. "How could you?"

"I was inebriated, Chrissy," sighed Mom. "If drunk me told him something I wasn't supposed to, you'll have to ask drunk me. Don't take it up with sober me, I wasn't there."

"Good morning, my lovelies!" trilled Grandma Helen merrily, as she walked through the back door. "Is it not an absolutely glorious day?"

"Ask me in about five hours," groaned Aunt Christine. "When I can function better."

"How are you not hungover, Mother?" asked Mom. "You were just as drunk as we were last night."

"Actually, no, dear, I wasn't," she smiled, walking over to them. "I hydrated and stopped drinking long before you. And it's a good thing too, Lord knows what kind of trouble the two of you would have gotten into if I hadn't." She grabbed a cup off the counter and grimaced when she saw them. "My God, have either of you looked in a mirror recently?"

"Don't need to," said Aunt Christine, shaking her head. "I'm pretty sure we look exactly the way we feel. But thanks for pointing it out as always, Mother."

"Hey, don't even act like you weren't hammered last night," sneered Mom. "You made everyone in that bar promise to join your obnoxious conga line when it came your time to sing *Copacabana*, or don't you remember?"

"Darling, I'm a performer, I don't need to be drunk to entertain a crowd," she smirked. "And, they gave me a standing ovation, or don't you remember?" She paused midway through pouring her coffee. "Oh, wait, you probably don't. I believe you were playing, 'What's my name' and losing by that point in the evening."

"Okay, well, it sounds like you ladies had an eventful evening last night," said Dad, turning to walk to his office. "Helen, I hope you took plenty of pictures."

"I'll be sure to text them to you, dear," she called out after him.

Leaning in close, she lowered her voice and raised her brow. "I believe I may even have a few of you fraternizing with that good-looking bartender, Christine. You know, the one who kept serving you all of those blowjob shots after tying your hands behind your back?"

"Please delete those, Mother," moaned Aunt Christine. "I really don't want a visual reminder of last night."

"But you looked so radiant last night," teased Grandma Helen. "Josh, the bartender certainly thought so. Tell me, did you end up calling him?"

"What?" exclaimed Aunt Christine. "Please tell me I didn't get his number."

"Well, you may want to consider how close the two of you became last night," she winked.

"Okay," interjected Ezra uncomfortably. "I wish I could say that I want to stay and hear more, but I really don't." He rinsed out his bowl and placed it in the dishwasher. "I think I'll just go ahead and leave while everything's still PG."

"It wasn't like that, Ezra," said Mom.

"So, what was it like?" I asked, sidling up to them. "And why were your hands tied behind your back?"

"It's just how you take the shot," answered Aunt Christine dismissively.

"No, it's not,' snickered Mom.

"It most certainly is!" she shot back. "I used to do them all the time back in college, and my hands were always behind my back."

"Behind your back, yes, but never tied," said Mom. "And certainly not with a silk scarf."

"You know, I wonder if he keeps that scarf handy for all of the drunk women that come into his bar?" wondered Grandma Helen aloud. "Or maybe just for the ones who flirt shamelessly with him."

Aunt Christine shifted uncomfortably in her chair. "Look, I may have had a bit too many, and I may have allowed myself to be a little too flirty, but I can assure you that I had absolutely no intention of taking it any further. I would never do something like that to Brian. I've been on the receiving end of that, remember?"

"Oh, honey, no one's suggesting you were going to," soothed Mom. "We were just giving you a hard time, and probably took it a little too far, that's all."

"Still, I would really appreciate it if you would please delete all of those pictures, Mom," said Aunt Christine. "I don't want Brian to see them and get the wrong idea."

"Oh, I didn't take any pictures, dear," scoffed Grandma Helen. "Well, at least not of the two of you, anyway. I did, however, get quite a few of me leading the conga line, and of my standing ovation, of course. But nothing else."

"Wonders never cease," snarked Mom, rolling her eyes.

"Anyway," continued Grandma Helen, ignoring the slight. "Now that we know that there's no evidence of your sister's debauchery, can we please go about our day?"

"What exactly did you have in mind?" asked Mom. "I don't think either one of us is up for much."

"Well, I thought I'd surprise all of you with a spa day," she smiled. "You know, massages, facials, mani/pedis, a day of pampering, if you will."

"Really?" I exclaimed. "That would be amazing, thank you!"

"Of course, my darling," she smiled. "And as for the two of you," she continued, pointing over at Mom and Aunt Christine, "Please try to make yourselves look presentable. This is a reputable spa, and I really don't want them thinking I'm doing some sort of rags-to-riches, charitable makeover."

"Gee, thanks, Mom," drawled Aunt Christine.

"Oh, and, for God's sake, take a shot of vodka, or something," snapped Grandma Helen, finishing her coffee. "It's quite honestly the only thing that's going to make you feel better."

"I don't think I can," said Mom, shaking her head. "I don't think my body's ready for that."

"Oh, don't be a baby, Olivia," scoffed Grandma Helen. "We've all been where you are right now, and we've all survived. You are no anomaly, my darling." She walked over to the back door, opened it, and resolutely called out, "Now, take the shot, clean yourselves up, and meet me outside in ten. The spa awaits."

Chapter Seventeen

It turns out that a day at the spa was exactly what everyone needed. Well, that and a shot of vodka. Of course, neither Mom nor Aunt Christine would ever admit to it, but that shot of vodka that Grandma Helen recommended had seriously revived them. So much so that they were able to enjoy a full day of pampering that included full-body massages, manicures, pedicures, and anti-aging facials. The two disheveled women, who had entered that salon looking like death had warmed over, came out three hours later looking relaxed, refreshed, and completely restored.

As we walked into the back room of Dante's, the host for Aunt Christine's bridal luncheon, we immediately saw that Nana and Nancy were busy setting things up for the afternoon. As they set out easels, paint pods, and paint brushes, they were talking and laughing as if they had known each other for years, which, of course, made Grandma Helen furious.

"Okay, what the hell is going on here?" she hissed, pulling Mom to the side. "The luncheon doesn't even start for another thirty minutes. Why is that loathsome woman already here?"

"I'm not sure, Mother, but if you'll release your death grip on my arm, I think we might just be able to find out," said Mom.

"And why are they laughing?" she pressed. "That woman is incapable of witty repartee, so what in the world could they possibly be laughing at?"

"Again, let go of my arm, and maybe we can find out," answered Mom.

"I'm sorry," said Grandma Helen, penitently, easing her grip. "I just can't seem to act like myself anytime she's around."

"And that's a bad thing?" snarked Aunt Christine.

"You know, I never should have encouraged you to speak," snarled Grandma Helen.

"Oh, stop it, Mother. I'm just kidding," she scoffed. "Come on, let's go see if they need any help."

"Ugh, must I?" sighed Grandma Helen. "I'd really rather just make myself a Bloody Mary."

"Okay, fine," said Mom. "Chrissy and I will go and help, then."

As we watched them make their way over to Nana and Nancy, Grandma Helen glanced around the room. "Darling, do you happen to know where the Bloody Mary bar is?"

"Didn't Mom tell you?" I asked. "Nancy's allergic to tomatoes, so they decided to go with a mimosa bar instead."

"They what?" she shrieked.

"Uh, they decided to do away with the Bloody Mary bar," I said uneasily. "Sorry, Grandma."

"Are you serious?" she exclaimed. "That was the whole point of having the luncheon here!"

"Okay, what exactly is your problem, Mother?" asked Mom, making her way back over to us. "Why are you so upset?"

"Oh, I don't know," exclaimed Grandma Helen. "Could it possibly be that the Bloody Mary bar I was so looking forward to has now turned into a mimosa bar?" She crossed her arms angrily over her chest. "Exactly when were you planning on telling me?"

"Would you please keep your voice down?" pleaded Mom. "You can still have a Bloody Mary, it's just that it's not going to be the main offering for the luncheon, that's all."

"That's all?" she repeated irritably. "We chose Dante's specifically for the Bloody Mary bar, remember?"

"No," answered Mom. "You chose Dante's for the Bloody Mary bar. Everyone else was perfectly happy to have this luncheon at Carol's, but you're the one who bulldozed your way into having it here." She softened her tone and then added, "However, that is not why we did away with the Bloody Mary bar. Nancy is allergic to tomatoes, and we thought it would be more hospitable if we had a safer alternative. Plus, Bloody Mary bars are known to get messy and tend to be a lot of work."

"How do we even know that she really has an allergy?" asked Grandma Helen. "She could be lying."

"And why would she do that?" asked Mom. "It makes no sense."

"It makes perfect sense when you're a bitch," she snapped back.

"Mother, please," said Mom. "I understand that you're upset, but let's try and get through this day without any bloodshed, okay?"

"Okay, fine," said Grandma Helen, irritably. "I'll just order my own damn Bloody Mary."

"Thank you," said Mom, sincerely. "Order as many as you want, and when you tire of those, you can just come over and help yourself to a mimosa. How does that sound?"

"It sounds like I just got screwed over for a woman who's incapable of being around a tomato," she snarked.

"Mom, please try to understand, we did this to make things easier," she said.

"Easier for whom, Olivia?" asked Grandma Helen, raising her brow. "You know what, it doesn't matter. This is my daughter's bridal luncheon, and if you want mimosas, then we'll have mimosas." She then raised her brow and grinned mischievously. "Although you may want to make sure that you keep Nancy as far away from me as possible. I would simply hate for a little drop of my tomato juice to accidentally make its way into her drink."

"Don't even think about it, Mother," warned Mom.

"Oh, please, I'm smarter than that, Olivia," she scoffed, turning to walk away. "I'm also very patient and equanimous and will more than happily wait for the right time to strike."

"What does equanimous mean?" I asked.

"Calm and composed," answered Mom.

"Oh, okay," I said. "She's kidding about the whole tomato juice in her drink, right?"

"For the sake of not having to come up with bail money, I certainly hope so," said Mom.

Thirty minutes later, we were smiling and welcoming the rest of Aunt Christine's wedding party. In addition to Mom and me, she had asked her two closest friends from New York, Crystal and Michelle, and her old college roommate, Poppy, to be her bridesmaids.

Poppy, who has always been on the heavier side, had earned the moniker, "Pudgy Poppy," years ago (unbeknownst to her) by Grandma Helen, after a brief meeting during parents' weekend of their freshman year.

"Okay, so, I see Michelle and Crystal, but where's Pudgy Poppy?" asked Grandma Helen.

"Please stop calling her that, Mother," snapped Aunt Christine. "It's not only rude, but completely unwarranted now that she's lost a good bit of weight."

"Darling, she would have to lose the equivalent weight of a Buick in order for that nickname not to fit," she snarked. "But, not to worry, I've already discussed damage control with the photographer, so disaster should be avoidable."

"You did what?" exclaimed Aunt Christine.

"Oh, calm down, Christine," dismissed Grandma Helen. "Someone had to do it."

"Mom, she is one of my best friends, and I will not allow you to ostracize her," she insisted. "Poppy will be treated like everyone else and will not be made a fool of, do you understand me?"

"Hey," soothed Mom, putting a hand on Aunt Christine's back. "Why don't you go and spend some time with Crystal and Michelle. I'll handle this."

"Thanks, Ollie," she smiled, meekly.

As soon as Aunt Christine was out of earshot, Mom immediately whirled around and scowled down at Grandma Helen.

"Okay, what exactly did you say to the photographer, Mother?" she asked.

"I simply told him that one of Christine's bridesmaids was fairly rotund and that we needed to find a way to make it so that she doesn't ruin all of the pictures," she answered innocently. "Your sister obviously won't allow me to place her somewhere inconspicuous, so I had to make the best of a bad situation."

"I see," said Mom. "And what, pray tell, is your solution to this supposed problem?"

"Well, I made mention of some specific posing options, camera angles, and then, of course, made sure that he had plenty of high-quality editing tools," she said. "We can't allow your sister's wedding pictures to look asymmetrical, now can we? It would completely ruin the aesthetic."

"Asymmetrical?" repeated Mom, in confusion. "What are you talking about?"

"Darling, there are five groomsmen and five bridesmaids, but adding Poppy into that mix is going to make it look like there are six bridesmaids because she takes up the space of two people," she answered irritably. "This way, we can at least edit her to make her look smaller, and thus, said symmetry will stay intact."

"Oh, my God, do you even hear the words that come out of your mouth?" asked Mom.

"Of course I do, dear," she replied cheerily. "I'm the one who's saying them."

Before Mom even had a chance to respond, Grandma Helen's attention shifted immediately to a strikingly beautiful woman who had just entered the room. She wore a high-end blush-colored pantsuit, expertly tailored to accentuate her petite waist, and her long auburn hair, which was tucked behind one ear, tumbled freely down the length of her back. The black Louboutin heels she wore, along with the matching clutch bag, completed the ensemble perfectly and made her look as though she had just stepped off a runway during fashion week.

Stepping further into the room, she carried a quiet and commanding elegance; however, beneath the polish, there seemed to linger a faint trace of uncertainty, almost as though she wasn't quite comfortable in her own skin.

"Who is that?" asked Grandma Helen.

"I have absolutely no idea," answered Mom.

"Well, she's obviously lost," she said. "I'll just go tell her that this is a private party and she'll need to see the hostess about getting a table."

"Oh, my God, Poppy, you're here!" squealed Aunt Christine, running over to embrace the new arrival. "I've missed you so much!"

"I'm sorry but have we just entered the *Twilight Zone*?" asked Grandma Helen. "There is absolutely no way that that's Pudgy Poppy. The last time I saw her, she was the size of a buffalo and had a rather large chocolate ice cream stain all over the front of her shirt."

"Well, she certainly doesn't look like that now, does she?" said Mom.

"That can't possibly be the same person," said Grandma Helen, shaking her head. "I mean, it just can't be. The woman standing over there is ethereal and graceful. Pudgy Poppy was corpulent and had a strange odor about her; they just can't possibly be the same person."

As Mom, Grandma Helen, and I made our way over to them, Aunt Christine began making introductions.

"Poppy, I'd like to introduce you to Michelle and Crystal, my two dearest friends from New York," said Aunt Christine. "They are the ones who helped me keep my sanity when Jack and I divorced."

"It's so nice to finally meet you," said Michelle, shaking her hand.

"We've heard so many wonderful things about you," added Crystal. "You look beautiful, by the way. I absolutely love your outfit."

"Thank you so much," smiled Poppy. "I've heard a lot about the two of you as well."

"And you remember my sister, Olivia," said Aunt Christine, gesturing toward Mom.

"Yes, of course, I do," she beamed brightly. "It's so good to see you again."

"You look absolutely amazing, Poppy," said Mom. "I'm so glad you could make it." She then turned and placed her arm around me. "I don't believe you've met my daughter, Addie. She's one of Chrissy's bridesmaids as well."

"Hi, Poppy, it's nice to meet you," I smiled, holding out my hand.

"I know we haven't met," said Poppy. "But your aunt speaks so highly of both you and your brothers. I'm so glad to finally have a chance to meet you in person."

"Oh, and this is Olivia's mother-in-law, Carol, and Brian's mom, Nancy," said Aunt Christine, redirecting the conversation. "And, of course, I'm sure you remember my mother, Helen."

"It's so nice to meet you," said Poppy, waving her hand over at Nana and Nancy. She then turned to face Grandma Helen. "And, Helen, it's so good to see you again. It's been way too long."

"Yes, it's lovely to see you too, dear," she smiled. "I think the last time I saw you was at Christine's last wedding, yes?"

"Yes, it was," she nodded. "It seems like a lifetime ago. So much has changed since then."

"Yes, well, I must say that I hardly recognized you when you walked through the door," admitted Grandma Helen. "You look entirely different from the last time I saw you."

"Well, I wear contacts instead of glasses now, and my hair is a good bit longer than it used to be," she pointed out. "And of course, I think I may look a little bit thinner than I did twenty years ago."

"A little bit?" challenged Grandma Helen. "Darling, you were the size of a house. You had a mortgage and a welcome mat."

"Uh, I'm sorry, what?" asked Poppy, a look of confusion contorting her face.

"Uh, believe it or not, that was a compliment," interjected Mom, quickly. "Mom tends to lose her sense of propriety whenever she's taken aback. I think your transformation has thrown her for a bit of a loop because it's such a miraculous one."

"Oh, well, thank you so much," smiled Poppy, uneasily. "I really appreciate it." She briefly glanced behind her and saw that everyone was gravitating over toward the tables. "Well, I guess I should go and join the others. It looks like they're getting ready to paint."

"Yes, you do that, dear," grinned Grandma Helen. "We'll be over there shortly."

As we watched Poppy make her way over to the rest of the group, Mom let out an irritable sigh.

"You know, you've really got to stop expressing every feeling you have every moment you have it, Mother," scolded Mom. "That could have ended in disaster."

"I don't see why," she shrugged. "I was giving her a compliment, just like you said."

"Telling someone that they were fat enough to have a mortgage and a welcome mat is not the way to get your point across," said Mom. "Not everyone thinks the way you do, and when you say things like that, it comes across like an insult. I'm just glad Chrissy didn't hear you. She would have been absolutely mortified."

"Oh, please, when has your sister not been mortified by the things that I say?" she scoffed. "Anyway, I think I've had about as much sober, female, bonding as I can manage, so I'm off to go and order myself a Bloody Mary. Would you like one, dear?"

"Uh, no, I'm good, thank you," said Mom, watching her strut away.

"You know, I think you deserve a medal," I said, putting my arm around her. "That was some quick thinking on your part."

“Thank you, honey,” she smiled, gratefully. “Now I just need to keep it up for the next three days without losing my sanity.” She took my hand and led me over to the mimosa bar. “But for now, I say we get ourselves a drink and brace ourselves for the next round.”

CHAPTER EIGHTEEN

"Oh, Nancy, that is really coming together nicely," said Nana, as she made her way around the room. "I see you took my advice about the flower."

"I did, yes," she nodded. "I had no idea that paint-by-numbers could be so much fun."

"Well, keep it up," encouraged Nana. "It's obvious that you have an excellent eye for detail."

"It's a paint-by-numbers," muttered Grandma Helen. "How much detail can there be?"

"Apparently very little if we're talking about yours," snarked Mom, looking over at her canvas.

"Oh, Crystal, I love that you decided to go with the coral rather than the apricot there," said Nana. "It really catches the eye."

"Thank you so much," she beamed. I decided to do what you said and branch out a little bit."

"Yes, me too," said Michelle. "Except I went with more of a magenta and lavender combination."

"Oh, that's a beautiful combination, Michelle," said Nana. "I can't wait to see how it all comes together."

"Exactly what is the point of a paint-by-numbers class, when you don't paint by the actual numbers?" hissed Grandma Helen. "For the life of me, I will never understand the allure of all of this. It's absolutely ridiculous."

"Shut up, Mother, and just paint your canvas," whispered Mom. "Better yet, have another drink and come back to it later."

"I don't want to come back to it later," she pouted. "I don't want to do this at all. I'm bored."

"Oh, Christine, I absolutely love the vibrant variations of yellow," said Nana. "It stands out so beautifully against the green of the leaves."

"Thank you, Carol," she smiled. "I can't believe how much fun this is."

"How that child came out of my body, I will never know," said Grandma Helen, shaking her head somberly. "The whole artsy fartsy, 'let's capture the narrative of the moment through art, completely eludes me."

"Gee, you don't say," said Mom, focusing on her painting. "And here I thought you were a regular patron of the arts."

"I appreciate the stage and being adored, dear," she pronounced proudly. "But outside of that, I couldn't care less. Honestly, I don't even think of acting as an art, but rather a way to gain attention."

"Well, at least you're honest about it," said Mom.

"That's really coming along nicely, Poppy!" exclaimed Nana, continuing to stroll around the room. "You know, a little bit of that Prussian blue might be a nice addition to the outside of those petals; maybe give them a little more definition."

"Oh, you're right, that would really look good," she said excitedly. "What a great suggestion."

"Am I the only one who thinks all of this is ridiculous?" sighed Grandma Helen.

"Yes," said Mom and me in unison.

"You know, if you actually tried putting in some effort, rather than complain the entire time, you might find that your painting doesn't look like something a preschooler has done," snarked Mom.

"Yes, well, it's called freedom of expression," snapped Grandma Helen. "It's idiomatic, metaphorical, and as of right now, a completed work."

"Whatever you say, Picasso," drawled Mom.

"Oh, Addie, I absolutely love these colors!" exclaimed Nana, walking over to us. She kissed me on the head and hugged me tight. "You make me so proud."

"And Olivia, yours is really coming along, too," she said, turning to face Mom's canvas. "Although you may want to think about adding a little bit of a darker green over the veins of the leaves. It'll help with the definition and make it a little more realistic."

"Okay, I will, thank you," nodded Mom.

"And let's see how you're doing, Helen," said Nana, sidling up next to her. "Did you decide to follow the color codes, or get a little creative and branch out on your own?" She stared awkwardly at the erratic painting standing before her. "Um, Helen, exactly how many Bloody Marys have you had?"

"I am not drunk, Carol," insisted Grandma Helen. "I just tend to get impatient with things like this; you know that." She stepped back and studied her painting carefully. "Honestly, I think it looks fine. Art is in the eye of the beholder, after all."

"Maybe if the beholder is blind, yes," said Nana.

"Listen, if that guy who threw paint all over the place can be considered a great artist, then so can I," she countered. "It's really not that difficult."

"You mean Jackson Pollock?" asked Nana.

"I don't know what his name was," sighed Grandma Helen irritably. "All I know is that his paintings always looked like a messy plate of nachos."

"Jackson Pollock was an Abstract Expressionist, Helen," said Nana. "His paintings were known to demonstrate emotion, energy, and subconscious movement. And yes, his work may have looked random and erratic, but studies have shown that his patterns contained intentional rhythm and structural complexity." She gestured toward Grandma Helen's painting and shook her head. "Yours is—"

"You know what, never mind," interrupted Grandma Helen. "I'll just order another drink and wait for everyone to be finished."

"Okay, suit yourself," smiled Nana pleasantly. "I'm going to see if anyone needs anything."

Grandma Helen plopped down in the chair and blew out an irritable breath.

"Oooh, I think someone just got schooled," taunted Mom playfully.

"Oh, shut up, Olivia," she snapped.

An hour later, once our paintings had dried, Nana lined them up along the far wall, arranging them in such a way that the restaurant began to resemble a makeshift art gallery. Every painting was proudly presented. Well, every painting except for Grandma Helen's, that is. Hers was currently lying face-down, sandwiched between an overly ripe trash bag and a stack of grease-stained cardboard boxes inside a dumpster behind the restaurant.

"You know, I still can't believe you made that poor waiter dispose of your painting, Mother," said Mom.

"Oh, he was perfectly happy to do it," said Grandma Helen dismissively.

"He didn't have any choice in the matter," said Mom. "You snatched it up and handed it over like it was an empty plate. What else was he supposed to do?"

"Honestly, darling, I really don't care," she smiled. "I'm just glad that portion of the afternoon has concluded. Besides, I have other things on my mind, anyway."

"Oh, this should be good," drawled Mom, rolling her eyes.

"How do you think she did it?" said Grandma Helen, staring over at Poppy.

"How did who do what?" asked Mom. "What are you talking about?"

"Pudgy Poppy," she clarified. "How do you think she lost all that weight?"

"You have got to stop calling her that, Mother," said Mom. "It no longer holds any credence."

"Yes, I can see that, dear," she said, studying Poppy intently. "But I'm curious, do you think she had some sort of gastric sleeve or gastric bypass done?"

"I have no idea," answered Mom.

"GLP-1?" asked Grandma Helen.

"Just stop," said Mom. "It's none of our business."

"Intermittent fasting?" she continued, ignoring Mom. "Liquid meal replacement? Prescription weight loss? Calorie deficit?"

"Why do you even care?" asked Mom. "It's not like you've ever taken an interest in Poppy before."

"Yes, but when someone loses that amount of weight, it tends to be an attention-getter," she said. "I'm simply being observant."

"Okay, yes, it has definitely caught my attention," agreed Mom. "But you've got to stop obsessing over it. If she wants to tell you, she'll tell you. But please stop staring at her, it's getting creepy."

We stood there silently sipping our mimosas when Grandma Helen proposed another question. "So, how much skin do you think they ended up cutting off her body?"

"Oh, my God, I'm done with this conversation," said Mom, walking away. "You seriously need help."

"You must be wondering the same thing, darling," said Grandma Helen, looking over at me. "I mean, it's kind of the elephant in the room, don't you think?"

"Maybe a little bit, yes," I confessed. "But not enough to make Poppy uncomfortable."

"Ugh, you're just like you're mother," she sighed irritably. "No fun, and entirely too unobtrusive."

"Most people would think that's a good thing," I said.

"No, most people are just too afraid to rock the boat, that's all," she countered. "It's a shame, really."

"So, Crystal and Michelle seem nice," I said, changing the subject.

"Oh, yes, they're lovely," smiled Grandma Helen. "Of course, Crystal's a bit of a trollop, and Michelle is a little too strait-laced, if you ask me, but together I suppose they strike a good balance."

"Trollop?" I asked. "What exactly do you mean by that?"

"Oh, you know, someone who sleeps with men casually," she said. "Someone who isn't always the most discreet when it comes to sexual relations."

"Wow, Crystal doesn't strike me as someone who would act that way," I said.

"Darling, that woman would spread her legs for a Twix bar," she snarked. "I shudder to think about how she's going to act with all of Brian's groomsmen."

"Grandma, that's a terrible thing to say!" I gasped. "Don't let Aunt Christine hear you say that."

"What? It's the truth," she shrugged innocently. "And how do you think I found out about it in the first place?" She leaned in closely and lowered her voice. "I mean, you should have seen her at Christine's last wedding; promiscuous, licentious, and completely indiscriminate. I'm quite sure each one of Jack's groomsmen left that weekend having climbed Mount Crystal."

"Okay, but that was over twenty years ago," I said. "People tend to do crazy things when they're young. I'm sure she has a better sense of propriety now that she's older."

"One can certainly hope," she sighed.

"Besides, all of Brian's groomsmen are married," I added. "I highly doubt anything like that will happen this time."

"Well, it certainly never seemed to stop her in the past, but perhaps you're right, maybe she's turned over a new leaf." She grabbed my hand and led me over to where everyone was sitting. "Come on, let's go see what they're talking about."

As we made our way over, we could hear everyone discussing this evening's plans.

"Okay, so we'll meet at the bar around 8:00," said Aunt Christine. "It's only going to be the bridal party and spouses, minus Ollie and Addie. They've decided to take it easy tonight."

"Oh, and I should probably tell you that Chris won't be there either," said Crystal. "He wasn't able to make it this weekend."

"Oh, no," said Aunt Christine. "Did something happen?"

"You could say that, yes," she said sheepishly.

"Is he sick or something?" asked Mom.

"No," she shook her head.

"Family emergency?" asked Michelle.

"Not quite, no," she answered tentatively.

"Oh, for God's sake, just spit it out, dear," spat Grandma Helen. "There's no need to draw it out."

"Mother, please," said Aunt Christine. "I'm sure she'll tell us when she's ready."

"Well, I suppose it's bound to come out sooner or later," said Crystal. She downed the last of her mimosa and then picked up another. "Chris just broke up with me."

"What? No!" exclaimed Michelle.

"Oh, honey, I'm so sorry," soothed Nana, placing her hand atop hers. "You know, I learned long ago that God often has other plans. I'm sure the right one is out there for you somewhere; you just need to give it some time."

"Yes, exactly," smiled Aunt Christine. "Look at Brian and me. We both had our hearts completely ripped out, but eventually that pain led us to each other, and now I couldn't be happier. So, yes, God's plans always work out for the best."

"Yes, well, I may have had a little something to do with him breaking up with me," sighed Crystal.

"I'll take cheating for $500, Alex," whispered Grandma Helen.

"Shh," I mimed, putting my hand to my lips.

"You know what, none of that matters," said Nancy. "The point is, you pick yourself up, dust yourself off, and get back out there. You can't let any of this nonsense deter you from living your life to the fullest."

"Thank you, Nancy, I really appreciate you saying that," smiled Crystal. She swallowed the second mimosa in one gulp and winced as it went down. "I honestly didn't think he'd find out."

"Find out what, dear?" asked Grandma Helen, nudging me playfully.

"That I slept with his brother," she sighed quietly.

"I'm sorry, what did you just say?" asked Nancy, taken aback.

"I slept with Chris' brother, and now he won't talk to me," answered Crystal. "It was wrong, I know that, and now I'm paying the price for it." She grabbed another mimosa. "And now, of course, his brother won't speak to me either, so I had no choice but to come here alone."

As we all took a moment to process what Crystal had just admitted, Grandma Helen smiled triumphantly over at me and whispered, "Told ya."

Chapter Nineteen

"She slept with his brother and is actually surprised that neither one of them wanted to come to the wedding with her?" asked Dad. "That's insane."

"I wouldn't say surprised, necessarily," answered Mom. "Maybe a little more inconvenienced than anything else."

"That's even worse," said Dad.

"And Grandma Helen totally called it, too," I added. "In fact, I think she was on the verge of taking bets, but I was able to dissuade her."

We had just finished cleaning up after dinner when Dad suggested we open a bottle of wine and bring him up to speed on all the afternoon's events. After filling him in on Poppy's dramatic weight loss, Grandma Helen's painting fiasco, and Crystal's confession of infidelity, it felt less like an ordinary family conversation and more like a summarization of a dramatic daytime soap opera.

"Well, Crystal's always been a bit loose," said Dad. "She's even hit on me a few times."

"She has?" asked Mom. "When?"

"At Jack and Christine's wedding," he answered. "Oh, and then again when we were all out at that bar in New York a few years ago." He took a sip of wine and grinned. "Of course, who could blame her? I am, after all, devilishly handsome and incredibly desirable."

"Wow, Dad, that's pretty brave of you to say out loud," snarked Beau, walking into the kitchen. "But, hey, self-care is important, so you just keep telling yourself that."

"Ha. Ha. Aren't you the funny one?" drawled Dad. He then turned his attention back to Mom and me. "And if Crystal is dumb enough to cheat on her boyfriend, especially with his brother, then she deserves what she gets."

"Ooh, who is this Crystal, and how can I meet her?" said Beau, trying to jam something into the dishwasher.

"I think she may be a little too old for you, dork," I said.

"Shut up, Addie," he spat.

"Okay, both of you stop right there," said Mom. "I am not in the mood to hear you argue tonight."

"You say that every time they argue," snickered Dad.

"Yes, well, that's because it happens all the time when you're not here," answered Mom.

"Ugh, Mom, I can't get this stupid thing to fit," huffed Beau, continuing to wrestle with the dishwasher.

"What, exactly, are you trying to put in there?" asked Mom.

"This stupid thermos," he said. "Oh. wait, there it goes."

"What thermos?" said Mom, getting up to see what he was doing.

"The one that Dad got from work," he said, lifting it up. "I used it for my hot chocolate this morning."

"Honey, that isn't dishwasher safe," said Mom. "You're going to have to wash it by hand."

He looked at the thermos and patted it softly. "I think you're going to be just fine, buddy. Do your best in there."

"Oh, no, you don't," said Mom, taking it from him. "This is going to get ruined if you put it in the dishwasher. If you had taken the time to read the bottom, you would see that it says, 'not dishwasher safe.'"

"Oh, ye of little faith, Mother," he said, shaking his head. "I'm simply trying to give the little guy a shot at debunking those so-called myths, that's all." He took the thermos from her and smiled. "And, as you've always taught me, sometimes we have to test things in order to prove them false. Think of it more as an impromptu science experiment than anything else."

"Oh, is that what this is?" she asked, suddenly interested. "Okay, well, in that case, go upstairs, grab your science book, computer, and a lab report. Don't forget to include the title of your experiment, the introduction and purpose, the materials and methods used, and then, of course, your final results. Oh, and also be prepared to discuss your interpretation, hypothesis analysis, error analysis, and anything else that may seem pertinent to your experiment."

"You know, now that I think about it, it may just be best if I go ahead and wash it while I'm down here," he said. "It is Dad's thermos, after all, and I certainly don't want to ruin it."

"How considerate of you," said Mom sarcastically.

"Son, has it ever occurred to you that doing the right thing in the first place, and not always trying to take the easy way out, is just a better way to do things?" asked Dad. "Not to mention the relief it would give your Mother to not have to watch everything you do all the time."

"Uh, not really, no," he answered frankly. "And, let's be honest, Mom's never not going to be watching over me. It's not in her nature."

"Oh, that reminds me," said Mom. "Please stop using our bathroom sink. You have your own bathroom to wash your hands. If you continue to keep using mine, I'm going to start charging you for it."

"Hey, I have a good reason for using your sink," he responded. "It's called "Operation We Don't Have Any Soap."

"Yes, you do," corrected Mom. "I put a brand-new dispenser up there last week."

"It's empty," he said.

"Then fill it up!" she exclaimed, beginning to lose patience. "There's a huge refill container underneath your sink."

"Uh, I'm sorry, but I think I'm going to have to stop you right there, ma'am," he said, holding up a hand. "I don't believe you've been given the clearance to instruct me to do that."

"Don't test me, Beau," muttered Mom calmly.

Seeing that she was not at all amused by his attempt at humor, he quickly changed strategy.

"Ma'am, yes, ma'am," he saluted her. 'Operation Fill Up the Soap' will commence in exactly zero point ten seconds."

"Thank you," she smiled. "And please try not to get it all over the sink."

"Yes, ma'am," he nodded.

"Hey, you know I love you, right?" she said, cupping his cheek.

"If I say no, do I still have to fill up the soap?" he grinned innocently.

"Go," she pointed toward the stairs. "And once you're done, you can have that last piece of pumpkin cheesecake you've been pining over."

"Sweet!" he exclaimed excitedly, running up the stairs. "Suck it, Ezra, that cheesecake is mine!"

Heaving a heavy sigh, Mom walked back into the living room. "Tell me, is it still considered neglect and abuse if I lock myself in the closet?"

"You let that boy antagonize you way too much," snickered Dad. "I think he does a lot of what he does just to mess with you."

"Yeah, I have to agree with Dad," I said. "You do tend to make yourself an easy target."

"That's easy for the two of you to say," she said, picking up her wine glass. "You're not the one who has to deal with him all the time."

Taking a sip of wine, she then gave Dad the side-eye. "So, exactly what did Crystal say when she was flirting with you?"

"It was a long time ago, Olivia," said Dad. "I honestly don't remember."

"Oh, come on, sure you do," she grinned. "Men always remember things like that."

"I really don't," he laughed, shaking his head. "But what I do remember, however, is thinking how gorgeous my wife is, and how happy I am to be able to spend the rest of my life with her."

"Nice save," she winked, pulling a blanket over her legs. "Still, the whole thing is kind of sad when you think about it."

"Another woman finding me sexy is sad?" snarked Dad, raising his brow. "Gee, honey, thanks for the vote of confidence."

"You know I didn't mean it that way," said Mom, looking over at him. "It's just that I find it kind of sad that at almost fifty, Crystal feels the need to act like she's still in her twenties." She stared into her wine glass and sighed. "Unfortunately, I think she's the type of woman who finds her worth and identity in the various men that she dates."

"Well, Aunt Christine seems to think that she secretly loves the drama of it all," I said. "That any attention, whether negative or positive, is what fuels her and makes her feel whole."

"When did she tell you that?" asked Mom.

"Today at the luncheon," I said. "She also said that she and Michelle are trying to persuade her to go into therapy. They think she may have some unresolved issues from a past trauma in her life."

"Oh, my God, are you serious?" said Mom. "And here I thought she was just acting like a slut."

"Who's acting like a slut, darling?" asked Grandma Helen, waltzing into the living room. "And is it someone I know?"

"How do you always manage to do that, Mother?" asked Mom.

"Do what, dear?" she smiled.

"Always walk in when we're talking about someone," said Mom. "It's uncanny."

"Oh, I don't know, divine intervention, perhaps?" she shrugged.

"Uh, I highly doubt that," laughed Dad, rolling his eyes. "Somehow I don't see God being that desperate."

"And, good evening to you, too, Gregory," said Grandma Helen wryly. "It's always so nice to receive such a heartfelt welcome."

"Oh, come on, Helen, you know I'm just kidding," winked Dad. "Why don't you come and join us for a glass of wine?"

"That would be lovely, dear, thank you," she smiled, taking a seat between Mom and me. "So, who are we talking about?"

"Crystal," we answered in unison.

"Oh, yes, that woman is definitely a tart," she nodded in agreement. "And probably has more frequent fliers than Delta and American Airlines combined."

"Grandma, that's a terrible thing to say!" I laughed.

"Well, if it walks like a duck…" she trailed off.

"She's apparently even tried coming on to Greg a few times," said Mom.

"No," whispered Grandma Helen in astonishment. "When did that happen?"

"The first time was at Jack and Chrissy's wedding," she answered. "And then the second time was when we were visiting Chrissy in New York. Can you believe she had the audacity to do that?"

"No, I can't," she shook her head. "What in the world could she have been thinking?"

"Oh, my God, why is it so hard for you people to believe that a woman would hit on me?" asked Dad, handing Grandma Helen a wine glass. "It's not like I look like the Elephant Man, you know."

"Oh, darling, that's not at all what I meant," she said, waving her hand dismissively. "I'm just surprised she would do something like that, knowing you're happily married to her best friend's sister. It's honestly quite brazen when you think about it."

"Do you think Aunt Christine knows that Crystal tried flirting with Dad?" I asked.

"I doubt it," said Mom. "She wouldn't keep something like that from me."

"Well, the woman obviously has no scruples," said Grandma Helen. "We may need to keep an eye on her. We certainly don't need to have another wedding with a nymphomaniac on the loose."

"Oh, I don't know," smiled Dad. "I think some of the men might actually like that."

The three of us just sat there silently and stared at him with a look of disgust.

"What?" he laughed. "Don't think for one second that there aren't men out there who wouldn't love to have a good-looking woman make advances on them."

Seeing that we had nothing to say, he continued to backpedal.

"Well, I certainly don't feel that way," he said defensively. "I'm just saying that some men might not be opposed to it, that's all." He took a sip of his wine and then added. "I mean, let's be honest, it's not like I'm telling you something you don't already know."

"Unfortunately, no, you're not, dear," said Grandma Helen. "We are all very aware that most men think with their—"

"Okay, let's just get back to the matter at hand, shall we?" interjected Mom quickly. "The fact is that none of us know, nor understand, what exactly is going on with Crystal. And we definitely need to avoid making assumptions about her behavior this weekend. The only thing we can do is wait to see how everything plays out, and then act accordingly."

"Alright, fine," shrugged Grandma Helen. "Let her go crazy and ruin your sister's wedding."

"I'm not saying that, Mother," said Mom. "I'm just saying that let's not cast aspersions when we don't even know what her intentions are. This whole thing with her boyfriend and his brother could have just been a complete lack of judgment on her part. We don't know."

"Oh, please," snickered Grandma Helen. "That woman doesn't just juggle men; she manages inventory."

"That may be the case," said Mom. "But it's none of our business, and we just need to keep out of it, okay?"

"Even if she tries coming on to me again?" taunted Dad. "I mean, that's certainly a possibility."

"I have complete trust in you, honey," smiled Mom.

"Oh, I don't think you have anything to worry about, Mom," I said. "Aunt Christine says Crystal's only into younger guys now, so that kind of eliminates Dad."

"Hey, I am not that old," he protested vehemently.

"Dad, your favorite thing to do is show everyone your socks whenever we go places and then tell them where they can buy them," I retorted sourly. "It's embarrassing."

"Okay, first of all, people absolutely love my sushi socks!" he said defensively. "And secondly, I know people are going to ask me where I get them, so I just save them time and tell them." He took a sip of wine and then added excitedly, "Wait until they see the ones I have with Churchill's face. People are going to love them!"

"I rest my case," I said, rolling my eyes.

Chapter Twenty

"Are you serious, right now?" exclaimed Ezra from the laundry room. He charged into the kitchen and held up his pants. "I can't believe you washed my clothes with the dog's bed!"

"Ezra, I have honestly lost count of how many times I've asked you not to use the washing machine as a laundry basket," said Mom. "And I absolutely refuse to take your clothes out when I have something quick I need to wash."

"But the dog's bed?" he said. "That's disgusting!"

"Well, you should have thought about that before you left your clothes in there," she shrugged.

"I only left them in there for a day," he answered defensively. "I was going to start a load when I got home."

"Yes, well, that didn't quite work out, did it?" she countered. "Besides, Churchill accidentally peed in his bed, and I needed to wash it so that he could have it for tonight while we're gone."

"Wait, you mean this wasn't just a maintenance cleaning?" he shrieked. "I don't have time to re-wash everything. I need my clothes for the rehearsal dinner."

"Again, you should have thought about that before leaving them in there," she said. "Besides, I don't know why you're so upset. I used plenty of soap and fabric softener."

"You use fabric softener for Churchill's bed," I asked. "Why?"

"He likes his bed to be soft, and I think the scent has a calming effect on him," said Mom. "Plus, I think it helps him sleep better."

I looked over at him snoring loudly on the hardwood floor. "Yeah, I really don't think he needs a laundered bed for that, Mom."

Ezra sniffed uneasily at his clothes and then held them out for Mom to smell. "Do you think they smell like dog?"

"No, Ezra," she sighed. "They don't smell like dog."

"What about pee?" he pressed.

"No," she answered, pushing the clothes away from her.

"Are you sure?" he asked. "I don't want Sabrina to be grossed out by the way my clothes smell."

Crossing her arms in front of her, Mom raised her brow and looked pointedly at him. "Ezra, you only just started regularly washing your socks and underwear a few months ago. If she hasn't fled by now, then I think you're safe."

"Oh my God, are you serious?" I curled my lip. "That is so gross."

Mom looked over at me and sighed, "Honey, a man's frontal lobe doesn't finish forming until he's approximately 25. This means that his decision-making, impulse control, and basic maturation will suffer until that time, so when you think about it, it's really not all that surprising."

"Yeah, well, it's still nasty," I said.

"On that, we can agree," nodded Mom.

"Okay, whatever," huffed Ezra, turning to go back upstairs. "I'm going to take a shower."

"Be sure to put on fresh underwear, socks, and deodorant when you're done!" she called out.

"Oh my God, I know what to do!" he yelled back. "I'm not a child!"

"He's right," smirked Mom, picking up her coffee cup. "Toddlers at least have the decency to own up to their tantrums."

"Hey, have either of you seen my phone anywhere?" asked Aunt Christine, walking into the kitchen. "I've been searching for it everywhere and can't seem to find it."

"You mean the one that's in your back pocket?" I laughed.

She reached behind and let out a huge sigh of relief. "Oh, thank God! I was starting to worry that I had left it at the bar last night."

"How was that, by the way?" asked Mom.

"I think it was good," she nodded distractedly. "Everyone seemed to have a good time." She looked through a few messages on her phone and then sat down. "We don't happen to have any vodka, do we?"

"Vodka?" said Mom, taken aback. "Whatever for?"

"I'm a little on edge and could really use something to calm my nerves," answered Aunt Christine.

"Why?" asked Mom. "What's going on?"

"Nothing yet," she shook her head, chewing on her nail nervously. "But I just know something bad is going to happen, like the flowers won't get there on time, or the preacher won't show up, or the walls at the reception hall are going to completely collapse around us." She looked worriedly over at Mom and me. "We have over 250 guests showing up tomorrow. What if everything completely falls apart?"

"Okay, you need to take a breath and calm down," said Mom, placing a hand on her arm. "Christian has double-and triple-checked, everything, and is very much in control of the situation. That is what you paid him for, remember?"

"Yes, but what if he misses something?" continued Aunt Christine. "Or what if everyone ends up getting food poisoning?" She looked up with a startled expression, and then added. "Oh my God, what if some sort of assassination squad guns down both Brian and me at the wedding rehearsal tonight?"

"Have you completely lost your mind?" asked Mom. "You're not making any sense."

"Look, I don't know, I'm just trying to prepare myself for different catastrophes," she sighed.

"I hate to tell you this," said Mom. "But you are not Uma Thurman, you are not a former assassin, and you are most certainly not living in the *Kill Bill* universe."

She pulled a wine glass down from a cabinet, filled it half-full of Merlot, and slid it in front of Aunt Christine.

"Here, drink this," she said. "You're starting to sound like Beau. And if there's one thing we don't need, it's another fantasist in this family."

"I do not sound like Beau!" she shot back.

"Assassins gunning you down at your wedding rehearsal?" said Mom. "Need I say more?"

"Alright, fair enough," she conceded. "I guess my imagination is running a little wild." She sipped her wine and then exhaled slowly. "It's just that I tend to stress about things before there are even things to stress about. And then I stress over things that don't even need to be stressed about, which then, of course, becomes stressful in and of itself." She opened her eyes. "Oh my God, I cannot stop stressing!"

"Okay, let's just slow down and look at this logically," offered Mom. "As far as all of the wedding day preparation goes, Christian has that completely under control. Also, I doubt you'll have anything to worry about with the catering. They have hosted hundreds of weddings, and I have never once heard of anyone getting sick. And as for your delusional *Kill Bill* fantasy, I'm fairly certain no one is intending in assassinating you or Brian at your rehearsal tonight." She pulled a wine glass out for herself and emptied the bottle of Merlot into it. "So you see, everything is going to work out just fine."

"And what about Mom?" she groaned. "You know that's always a catastrophe waiting to happen."

"She can be unpredictable, yes," nodded Mom. "But she has assured me that she will be on her best behavior this weekend."

"Unless she's not," muttered Aunt Christine quietly.

"Look, you can either sit here worrying about every single scenario that may or may not happen," said Mom. "Or you can look forward to spending the weekend in celebration, knowing that at the end of it, you're going to be happily married to the man of your dreams. The choice is yours." She lifted her glass and inhaled deeply. "Just know that it's going to be what it's going to be, and that lamenting over things you can't control is only going to drive you crazy."

"You're right," she agreed. "I'm being ridiculous."

"Hey, it's a big weekend for you, I get it," smiled Mom. "But just know that we're here for you and will do everything in our power to make it as perfect as possible."

"Thanks, Ollie," said Aunt Christine. "I can always count on you to help me see reason." She looked up at the time and practically choked on her wine. "Oh, my God, I have to get ready!" She jumped out of her seat excitedly and ran out of the kitchen. "I can't believe by this time tomorrow I'm going to be Mrs. Brian Caldwell!"

Mom and I smiled in amusement as we watched her leave.

"I'm so happy she finally found her person," I said. "She and Brian are a perfect for each other. I can't wait to see what the future holds for them."

"Most likely it's going to be a future that's filled with great happiness, petty of arguments, and the occasional Mexican standoff."

"Mexican standoff?" I asked.

"Oh, you know, when you're having an argument with someone and become irritable because the other person is irritable," she said. "And then your irritability increases because the other person refuses to stop being irritable. And, since you know full well that the other person isn't going to apologize, you become even more irritable because you know that you're the one who's going to have to do it. Of course, once you finally do offer up the apology, you find yourself suffering through your irritability quietly because you just apologized for something you're really not sorry for."

"I'm sorry, but could you please explain that to me in English?" I said.

"Let me give you an example," she smiled. "I remember fighting with your father one time after we were first married. I don't remember exactly what we were fighting about, but I do remember being really hungry, mentally exhausted, and wanting the whole thing to be over. So, rather than continuing to fight, I just decided to be the one to bite the bullet and apologize. I didn't really mean it, of course, but he certainly didn't know that. Twenty minutes later, we found ourselves eating tacos and drinking margaritas, and acting like the fight had never even happened." She sipped her wine and then added, "And, that, my dear girl, is why you'll usually find that it is women who waive the white flag first. You see, they're mature enough, and smart enough, to realize that peace is much easier to live with than strife."

"Do you think that happens in every marriage?" I asked.

"Oh, I know it does," she laughed heartily. "Women talk about it all the time. It's like we're members of some special club where we all share the same frustrations." She picked up the empty wine bottle and tossed it into the trash. "And then one day, you'll eventually find yourself trailing behind your husband through a Home Depot for forty-five minutes, trying not to kill him, when you look across the aisle and lock eyes with another forlorn woman who's suffering the same fate. And it's at that very moment that you immediately come to realize that you're both part of the exact same club."

"And what club is that?" I asked.

"Well, in that particular case, it's a club where you stand idly by and watch your husband purchase supplies for a project that won't actually get started for another two years."

Taking my silence as a cause for concern, she softened her voice and continued. "Marriage is not perfection, Addie; it's patience. It's two people deciding that, despite life's many ups and downs, it's more important to face it together rather than separately. It's ordinary mornings, long years, and the slow passing of time. It's also the comfort of having someone who knows all of the unpolished parts of you; the moods, the worries, the strange habits, and yet, still continues to love you despite them." She laughed quietly to herself. "It's someone who surprises you with a high-velocity, portable, utility fan for your bedroom because he knows how bad your hot flashes can get or decides to buy you a 3000-piece rotating puzzle board because you mentioned in passing that your neck hurts after piecing together a puzzle."

"So, it's doing life together," I smiled.

"Exactly," she nodded.

"I see that a lot with you and Dad," I said. "You both always seem happy together."

"Well, after 28 years of good times and bad times, I can honestly say that he is still my favorite person to spend time with," she grinned. "Plus, it helps that he's easy on the eyes."

We were just about to get up and get ready for the wedding rehearsal when Grandma Helen burst through the back door.

"Tell me, am I the only person running out of people I like?" she huffed.

"Considering there are fewer than a handful of them, yes," snickered Mom. "So, who's upsetting you today, Mother?"

"Margaret Miller," she snarled.

"Who's Margaret Miller?" I asked.

"Someone who is now dead to me," she answered, folding her arms in front of her.

"Margaret is one of the board of directors for the theater," clarified Mom. "She's actually a very lovely woman."

"She's a traitor," said Grandma Helen firmly.

"And what did she do to earn that moniker?" asked Mom.

"She changed her vote," she snapped. "We were all set to vote on *Moulin Rouge!* for our next production, but this afternoon, she changed her mind. And, since she was the deciding vote, we're now stuck having to do *Little Shop of Horrors.*" She slammed her hand down on the counter. "I hate that show!"

"Have you ever seen it?" asked Mom.

"Well, no, but that's not the point," she said dismissively.

"Why do you think she changed her mind?" I asked.

"Apparently, she decided that *Moulin Rouge!* was just too risqué for local theater, and unsuitable for anyone under the age of 12," she said, rolling her eyes. "Ugh, I could just kill her!"

"Well, maybe she has a point," said Mom. "It is community theater, after all. If the whole community can't attend, then it's really not for the community, you know?"

"Darling, the youngest actor we have in our ensemble is Michael, who is 61," she countered. "So do you really think anyone under the age of 50 attends our shows?"

"Okay, that's a fair point," said Mom. "But, you never know, *Little Shop of Horrors* could be fun."

"Yes, and so can doing taxes, if you're delusional enough." She walked back toward the door. "Anyway, I can't think about this now, I'll have to think about it later."

"Okay, but just know that if you end up getting the part of Audrey II, you'll have the best lines of the entire play," said Mom.

Stopping dead in her tracks, she slowly turned back toward Mom. "Is that the little plant thingy?"

"It is, yes," nodded Mom. "She's also the most popular character, too."

"Well, perhaps I may look a little more into it, then," she said. "I am nothing if not versatile."

We watched her walk out the door and then I said. "You pretty much just pulled that out of thin air, didn't you?"

"It's all about painting things in a certain light when it comes to your grandmother, Addie," said Mom. "If something can place her at the center of everyone's attention, it will immediately become desirable. I guess you could say it's her kryptonite."

"How long do you think it'll take before she changes her tune?" I asked.

"The very minute she realizes that someone else wants that part," she drawled.

Chapter Twenty-One

"Hey, you never told me these people were loaded!" exclaimed Beau, as we entered the large, wrought iron gates to the Caldwell's house.

"I didn't realize I needed to," said Mom.

"You're kidding, right?" he said, staring out the window in complete awe. "So, with Aunt Christine marrying into all of this, does that mean we become rich by proxy now?"

"I see you've been keeping up with the boy's vocabulary lessons," muttered Dad, as he drove along the sleek, oak-lined road.

"It's one of the few times he actually listens to me," drawled Mom, rolling her eyes. She turned around and looked at Beau. "And, no, this doesn't mean we're rich now."

"But we're going to be related," pressed Beau. "Shouldn't that stand for something?"

"You can't honestly believe we're entitled to a portion of the Caldwell's wealth simply because your aunt is marrying into the family," said Mom. "That would be inane."

"I don't know what that word means, but if it gets me money, then I'm fine with it," he said.

"It means silly and senseless," I said. "Which, you are both."

"Shut up, Addy," he snarled.

"You know, son, money doesn't always buy happiness," said Dad. "There are a lot of people out there with plenty of money who are morbidly depressed and miserable."

"Okay, well, those people are obviously using money wrong, then," he snarked.

As we made our way around the final bend of the long, winding driveway, Tim and Nancy Caldwell's home immediately came into view. It was a sprawling white Southern estate, complete with a wide wraparound porch, tall vertical windows, and grayish-blue shutters, that instantly brought to mind images of the fictional home, Tara, from *Gone with the Wind.*

The property surrounding the home was equally stunning with perfectly trimmed hedges and curving stone pathways that weaved in and around quaint gardens filled with a variety of vibrant plants, including lavender, roses, and hydrangeas. It was definitely a place that screamed wealth, but not necessarily in an ostentatious manner.

"There you are," greeted Tim, opening the front door. "We were beginning to worry that you'd gotten lost."

"Sorry about that," smiled Dad. "We ran into some old friends just as we were leaving and ended up talking with them for a bit."

"Well, you're here now, so come on in and join the festivities," he said.

Upon entering the grand foyer, Beau let out a low whistle. "Man, this house is nice, Mr. Caldwell."

"Thank you, Beau," he smiled. "We've lived in this house for thirty years, so we've had a lot of time to work on it." He gestured toward the back of the house. "Come on, I'll take you out back to where the party is."

Beau looked up at the enormous crystal chandelier hanging above and leaned in close to Mom. "Hey, maybe we should think about getting one of those for our entryway. You know, spruce it up a bit, and make it look a little fancier."

"Beau, that thing wouldn't fit in our living room, let alone our entryway," she said. "And for the record, this is a foyer."

"What's a foyer?" he asked.

"It's an area that serves as a transition into the home," she said. "They're usually larger spaces that are decorated with accent tables, chandeliers, and artwork, much like this one is."

"Well, whatever it is, it's got me thinking you and Dad need to make some serious upgrades," he countered. "Or better yet just buy a nicer house."

"And how would you suggest we do that?" asked Mom.

"I don't know," he shrugged. "Maybe Dad could get a side hustle doing some insider trading or pulling off a few bank heists, or maybe you can start selling Essential Oils."

"You really need to work on getting a better understanding of how life works," she laughed.

"So, I take it that's a no?" he asked.

"It's a resounding no," she said.

"Okay, fine, but some people earn pink Cadillacs selling that stuff," he said.

"That would be Mary Kay," she clarified. "And before you say anything, I'm not interested in selling that either."

As we followed Tim through the house, we were stunned by how beautiful it all looked. Every space felt meticulously curated with layers of texture, color, and light. The walls were dressed in rich tones and tasteful art, and the furniture was perfectly arranged with effortless precision. Each room carried its own distinct character, and they weren't just elegant but were composed, refined, and undeniably expensive. The Caldwell's home didn't simply suggest luxury, it fully embodied it, right down to the most minute detail.

Eventually, Tim led us to a set of French double doors that opened out onto a massive patio where lanterns traced the edge of multiple gardens. Several round tables decorated with crisp, white linens, polished silver, and striking floral arrangements sat sporadically around the large space.

The entire wedding party was present, laughing and conversing over the soft strain of music playing in the background. It was a truly beautiful space and served as the perfect setting for Brian and Aunt Christine's rehearsal dinner.

"Oh, my God, you're finally here!" exclaimed Aunt Christine. "Where have you been?"

"We got tied up talking with some friends back at the Laurel Estate," said Mom. Leaning in close, she added, "I remember you saying Brian's family had money, but this is beyond what I had imagined."

"It's a bit extravagant," she agreed. "But they mean well."

"Is Brian okay with all of this?" asked Mom.

"I think he's going to have to be since the evening's already started," she laughed.

"That's not what I meant," replied Mom.

"I know," laughed Aunt Christine, pulling a champagne flute from a waiter's tray. "And to answer your question, no, he's not at all comfortable with any of this. Brian doesn't like to flaunt his wealth like his parents do, which is why he's always chosen to live much more conservatively."

"Well, if he doesn't want it, I'll be happy to take it," said Beau.

He looked to his right and immediately locked eyes with a table piled high with chilled shrimp, raw oysters, and cracked crab claws.

"Man, I love people with money," he sighed contentedly. "I'll be over at the seafood bar if anyone needs me."

"Don't be gluttonous," called out Mom. "And be sure to leave something for the rest of the guests."

"I can make no promises, Mother," he quipped, heading for the table.

"God, I hope he doesn't make himself sick," she sighed. "That child has absolutely no control when it comes to any type of buffet."

"Don't worry, I'll keep an eye on him," said Dad, following behind.

"Thanks, honey," she smiled. "Oh, and remember, you need to coordinate with Dad and Ezra about picking up your tuxes tomorrow."

"Will do," he nodded.

"I can't believe how beautiful all of this is," I smiled, admiring the lights and table settings. "It looks like something that would be in a movie."

"And there's not an assassin in sight," added Mom sarcastically.

"Thank you, Addie, but I can't take credit for any of this," she said. "This was all Nancy's doing." She peered over at Mom. "And as for assassins, I think we might just be in the clear. I still can't believe I let imagination get away from me like that."

Aunt Christine looked up and saw that Brian was waving her over.

"Hey, Brian needs me, do you mind if I catch up with you later?" she asked.

"Of course," smiled Mom. "You go do what you need to do, we'll be fine." She lifted two glasses of champagne from a waiter as he walked by and handed one to me. "Well, we may as well get started."

As we stood toasting the couple of the hour, Grandma Helen hurriedly walked up beside us.

"I've been looking all over for you," she hissed. "Where have you been?"

"Oh, sorry, we were running a bit late," said Mom. "Is everything okay?"

"I don't know," she said. "But I think Nancy's up to something."

"Oh, come on, Mom, that's ridiculous," she said. "She's entirely too busy playing hostess to be up to anything."

"Oh, no, no, no, my darling," snickered Grandma Helen, sipping her martini. "I'm telling you, that woman has something up her sleeve. I can just feel it."

"Tell me, is your Spidey-sense tingling again, Mother?" joked Mom.

"Make fun of me all you want, dear, but I'm rarely wrong about these things, and you know it," she shot back.

"And what, exactly, has she done to make you think this?" asked Mom.

"She keeps looking over at me with a really smug look on her face, like she knows something I don't," she snarled. "It's unsettling."

"I think you're being paranoid," said Mom. "I'm sure she's just—"

"Did you see that?" gasped Grandma Helen, cutting her off. "She just did it again!"

"I didn't see anything, Mother," answered Mom.

"Addie, please tell me you saw that," said Grandma Helen beseechingly.

"I'm sorry, Grandma, but I didn't see anything either," I shrugged apologetically.

"Damnit," she sighed heavily, sipping her martini. "I just don't understand how people don't see her true colors. The woman is as fake as they come."

"You know, just because the two of you don't get along, doesn't mean she's a bad person," said Mom. "And no, other people may not see what you think you see, but that's not necessarily a bad thing."

"Darling, I may not be good at fractions, but it doesn't take a mathematician to see that she is one whole bitch," she spat.

"You've really got to stop with all of this vitriol toward Nancy," said Mom. "We are here for Brian and Christine, remember? This whole vendetta you've made up in your head needs to be placed on hold, at least for the remainder of the weekend, okay?"

"Then tell her to stop looking smugly at me," she answered defiantly, crossing her arms. "It's rude and completely uncouth."

"Mother, just let it—"

"Oh, my God, she did it again!" erupted Grandma Helen. "Did you see it that time?"

"Uh, yeah, I actually did," said Mom dubiously.

"See? I told you!" she hissed. "I knew I wasn't losing my mind."

Just as Mom and I were about to explain to Grandma Helen that Nancy wasn't plotting anything against her, Tim began clinking his glass to get everyone's attention.

"Excuse me, everyone," he smiled. "I hope you don't mind, but Nancy and I would like to say a few words to our son and his beautiful bride-to-be."

He beckoned for Brian and Christine to join them over by one of the tables and set down his glass.

"Brian, Christine," he began slowly. "Tomorrow is going to be the easy part. The vows, the ceremony, the applause, that's all fun and wonderful, but it's the life that you build together afterward that really counts."

He gazed over at Brian. "Son, I've watched you grow into an amazing man, and there is absolutely no doubt in my mind that you will be an amazing husband as well." He laughed inwardly and then said, "It's funny, when you told your mother and me that you had reconnected with an old high school friend, someone you hadn't seen in decades, we weren't quite sure what to think, but your mother and I couldn't be happier for both of you."

Turning to Christine, he smiled warmly. "And you, my darling daughter-to-be, have done something absolutely remarkable. You stepped into my son's life and made him calmer, steadier, and happier. You didn't just complete him, you enhanced him, and Nancy and I will be forever grateful for that."

He paused momentarily and reached into his pocket. "Nancy and I wanted to give you something special to commemorate this wonderful occasion. We know that starting a life together can be complicated, so we decided to ease your burden a little."

He held up a small keyring. "Recently, you were upset to find out that your dream home had been sold out from under you. Well, please don't be angry, but we're the ones who bought it out from under you."

He handed them the keyring and placed his arm around Nancy. "And now we'd like to give it to you as a wedding gift."

Grandma Helen choked on her drink and stood completely motionless, as a look of pallor spread across her face.

"Oh, my God!" exclaimed Brian. "Mom, Dad, thank you!"

"I can't believe you did this for us," cried Aunt Christine, hugging them tightly. "I don't even know what to say."

"Holy crap, did they literally just gift them a house?" asked Ezra, walking up to us.

"What a lovely gesture," smiled Sabrina.

"It really is," I agreed. "That was so nice of them."

Mom saw the look of shock on Grandma Helen's face and immediately put an arm around her.

"Hey, are you okay?" she asked.

"I can't believe they did that," she said quietly. "That's why she was looking at me the way she was. She knew what they were planning to do."

"We don't know that," said Mom. "This is just—"

"Yes, we do," said Grandma Helen somberly. "She knows full well I can't compete with a house."

"Mom, this isn't a competition," she said gently. "Christine and Brian aren't those kinds of people, you know that."

"Yeah, well, remind them of that when they open the espresso machine your father and I bought them," she murmured gloomily. "Excuse me, but I think I need to use the restroom."

"Mom, please don't go," she called out after her. "Let's talk about this."

"I think you need to give her a little bit of time, Mom," I said. "This is obviously hard for her."

"I suppose you're right," she sighed. "I just didn't expect that kind of reaction from her."

"Now that's what I call a gift!" exclaimed Beau, sidling up next to Mom. "I'm serious, if those people are looking to adopt, I am more than willing to volunteer."

"Yeah, well, I'm pretty sure you'd be returned in less than a week," drawled Mom.

"I'm not so sure about that," he grinned. "You know how charming I can be whenever I put my mind to it."

"Ugh, you are entirely too covetous," I said with disgust. "It's sad, really."

"Say what you will, dear Sister," he responded smugly. But I am more than happy to change my last name to Caldwell if it means getting a high-interest savings account and a trust fund." Picking up an enormous shrimp, he doused it in cocktail sauce and added, "Yeah, I could definitely get used to this."

Chapter Twenty-Two

"Olivia, honey, have you seen your mother?" asked Grandpa Anthony. "I can't seem to find her anywhere."

"No, I figured she was with you," said Mom.

"I lost track of her after Tim's toast," he said. "I've looked everywhere in the house for her and she's nowhere to be found." He lowered his voice and then added, "I think she might be a little upset about what happened."

"You mean about the house?" she asked.

"Yes," he nodded. "I could tell she wasn't acting herself after that, but figured she'd bounce back like she normally does."

"Hey, Anthony, are you going to be joining us?" asked Dad, placing a hand on his shoulder. "A bunch of us are heading down to the firepit for cigars. Tim's bringing out his Cubans."

"Ugh, I hate the smell of cigars," I said, curling my lip. "They're so pungent."

"Which is why we're smoking them down there and not up here," said Dad. "We don't want to offend any of you ladies." He paused momentarily. "Well, most of you, anyway. Crystal, Nancy, and Sabrina will be joining us."

"I thought Cubans were illegal in the United States," said Mom.

"Well, I won't tell if you won't," winked Dad. "Besides, someone's got to keep an eye on Crystal, right?"

"And you thought you'd be the one to volunteer as tribute, is that it?" drawled Mom sarcastically.

"It's a sacrifice I'm willing to make," grinned Dad, pulling Mom in close and kissing her. "Of course, you're more than welcome to come and keep an eye on me, if you'd like."

"I think I'll pass," she said. "I don't care for the smell of cigars either."

"Hey, Dad, are you coming?" asked Ezra excitedly. "Tim's got a bourbon bar down there too!"

"Sorry, honey, but duty calls," said Dad, leaving to follow Ezra. "Anthony, are you coming?"

"Uh, yeah, just give me a few minutes," answered Grandpa Anthony hesitantly.

We could see that he was torn between continuing to look for Grandma Helen and having cigars with the guys, so Mom went ahead and made the decision for him.

"Go have fun with the guys," she smiled encouragingly. "Addie and I'll go and look for Mom."

"Are you sure?" he said. "I don't mind helping you look for her."

"Come on, Anthony!" called out Tim. "I've got a Cuban with your name on it."

"Go," said Mom, nudging him to follow Tim. "We'll find Mom."

"Okay. Thanks, honey," he smiled. "Let me know when you find her, okay?"

"I will," she nodded.

I watched him catch up to everyone and then sidled up to Mom.

"So, where do you think Grandma went off to?" I asked. "Should we be worried?"

"No," said Mom, shaking her head. "She's probably just found someplace quiet to lick her wounds, that's all."

We spent the next twenty minutes searching the entire house but came up empty. On a whim, Mom suggested that we take a look out by the gardens, and that is exactly where we found her, her silhouette still and unmistakable along the curve of a nearby path.

"Jesus, there you are," said Mom, walking up to her. "Dad's been looking all over the place for you, and so have we. Why are you standing out here?"

"I wanted to be alone," she answered somberly.

Mom glanced briefly at the multiple wisteria trees, hydrangeas, and roses surrounding them. "And this is where you chose to come?" she asked.

"Yes," said Grandma Helen. "Is there a problem with that?"

"Uh, no," said Mom. "It's just that you tend to hate being around plants, flowers, or any type of botanical setting that requires you to be outdoors."

"No, dear, what I hate is not being able to punch Nancy Caldwell in the throat," she snarled viciously. "And, since doing so would have most likely been frowned upon, I decided to remove myself from the situation."

"Well, thank God for that," said Mom. "An arrest for assault would not be the best way to start this weekend's festivities."

"It'll make one hell of an end to it, though," muttered Grandma Helen quietly.

"Grandma, you don't mean that," I said. "You would never physically hurt anybody."

"Yes, well, I'm more than willing to make an exception when it comes to that godawful woman," she retorted.

"Okay, what's going on?" asked Mom. "You're obviously upset about something."

"I'd rather not talk about it," she sniffed.

"The fact that you're standing out here alone in a garden, of all places, tells me that you most definitely need to talk about it," said Mom. "Not to mention Christine will eventually begin to wonder where you are."

"I highly doubt that," she snorted. "I'm sure I'm the furthest thing from her mind right now.

"That's not true, and you know it," said Mom. "She would never—"

"I'm losing her, Olivia!" she cried out. "And that loathsome woman and that damn house are the reasons why!"

"Mom, you are never going to lose her, I promise," said Mom, hugging her tightly. "Chrissy loves you so much, she would never do something like that to you."

Grandma Helen stood back and let her tears fall.

"You and I have always been close, Olivia," she said, wiping the tears away. "And that closeness grew even more after your father and I moved in next to you. However, Christine has always been somewhat elusive. She's traveled the world once over and has lived in New York most of her life, so I never really had the opportunity to spend a lot of time with her.

I was hoping that once she moved back home, I'd have a chance to reconnect with her; maybe even have the kind of relationship I have with you. But now, I'm competing against Nancy, who has more money than God, and there's no way I can win against that."

"Oh, Grandma, you can't think that way," I said, putting my arm around her. "You're her mother, and she absolutely adores you. No amount of money will ever change that."

"Addie's right," said Mom. "You can't think that like that. Christine is not going to push you aside just because Nancy's in her life. I mean, will she spend time with her? Yes. Will she stop spending time with you? No."

She pulled out a small compact from her pocket and handed it to Grandma Helen. "Besides, Nancy may be rich, but she's got nothing on you," she smiled.

"She doesn't?" sniffed Grandma Helen, opening the compact.

"No," answered Mom. "She doesn't have your passion, enthusiasm, or zest for life." She cleaned away a small smudge under Grandma Helen's eye. "And if I'm being honest, she's one of the most boring people I've ever met."

"She is rather drab, isn't she?" she said, inspecting her reflection in the small mirror.

"And, here's something you probably didn't know," continued Mom. "She doesn't really like Neil Diamond."

"What?" she shrieked. "Who doesn't like Neil Diamond?"

"Apparently Nancy," answered Mom. "She had the opportunity to meet him in person after one of his concerts, and when he asked her what she thought of the show, she said, and I quote, that it was okay."

"Okay?" she repeated, lowering the compact. "She had the audacity to tell Neil Diamond that his show was okay?"

"As I said, she's not a big fan," shrugged Mom.

"Not a fan?" reiterated Grandma Helen angrily. "Neil Diamond is one of the greatest entertainers of all time. He is a prolific composer, songwriter, and singer, and his music has cross-generational appeal. People of all ages, and from every corner of the world, attended his concerts. The man's a national treasure, for God's sake!"

"I agree with you," said Mom. "I've always loved his music, you know that."

"I love his music too," I smiled. "One of my favorite memories is Mom playing *Sweet Caroline* for me when I was little."

"That's because your mother has taste, dear," she said, lifting the compact back up. "So, how exactly did you find out this information?"

"Christine told me when we were talking to the DJ about what kind of music to play," answered Mom. "She couldn't believe it either." She crossed her arms over her chest and smirked wickedly. "And you'll never believe who she actually does like."

"Who?" we asked in unison.

"The Carpenters," said Mom.

"Oh my God, that explains so much," sneered Grandma Helen.

"I thought you'd like that," laughed Mom.

"Ugh, I can't stand the Carpenters," she shuddered. "Christine had better not be planning on playing any of their songs at the wedding."

"No," chuckled Mom. "She hates them just as much as you do."

"Oh, thank God for small mercies," she sighed in relief. "I don't think I can take dealing with both the Carpenters and Nancy all in one day."

Grandma Helen took one final look in the small mirror and handed the compact over to Mom.

"Well, I suppose we should get back to the party," she sighed. "I'm sure Nancy's already set up a huge projector screen showcasing every aspect of the new house they bought for them."

We followed Grandma Helen through the house and then onto the back patio.

"Where have you been?" asked Aunt Christine. "I looked for all of you down by the firepit, but none of you were there."

"Oh, we decided to take a walk through the front gardens," smiled Mom. "They're absolutely beautiful, by the way."

"And you willingly went with them?" she asked Grandma Helen pointedly.

"Yes, well, I was in need of some fresh air," she said.

"We're already outdoors, Mother," drawled Aunt Christine. "You're literally surrounded by it."

"You know, I think I'm going to go see what your father's up to," said Grandma Helen, ignoring the wisecrack. "I haven't seen much of him tonight."

Aunt Christine watched her walk away and immediately looked over at Mom.

"Alright, what's going on?" she asked. "That woman would never willingly step foot into a garden or any space that supports nature."

"Give her a break, Chrissy," said Mom warily.

"Okay," she drawled. "And since when do you not like taking a good jab at Mom?"

"Since we found her standing alone out in the garden crying," answered Mom. "She was really upset."

"Wait, what?" said Aunt Christine, shaking her head in disbelief. "Why?"

"I think Tim and Nancy's elaborate wedding gift caught her a little off guard," said Mom. "It made her feel like she can't compete with them."

"Why in the world would she want to compete with them?" asked Aunt Christine. "That makes absolutely no sense."

"Maybe not to you, but it does to her," she snapped.

"Okay, I'm sorry," said Aunt Christine defensively. "You don't need to get snippy with me."

Mom released a breath and then softened her tone.

"Look, I'm sorry, I shouldn't have lashed out at you like that," she said. "It was just really hard to see Mom so upset."

"It's okay, I understand," said Aunt Christine, giving a reassuring smile. "What I don't understand is why she even feels the need to compete with Tim and Nancy."

"Chrissy," said Mom softly. "Imagine having to attend your daughter's rehearsal dinner at the home of the one person you dislike most in this world. And it's not just any home, either. It's an opulent and luxurious estate that exudes enormous wealth and affluence. Then, without warning, that same person and her husband present your daughter with a gift so extravagant it doesn't even seem real. And the fact that it was offered so casually, like it was absolutely nothing, makes it even worse because you know you'll never be able to buy your daughter anything like that. So you smile. You say the right things. And then you slip away quietly before anyone, especially her, can see how you really feel, which is embarrassed, defeated, and discouraged."

"Is that really what she was thinking?" whispered Aunt Christine worriedly.

"Well, that, and that she thinks she's going to lose you," answered Mom.

"Lose me?" she said. "She's never going to lose me."

"That's what I told her, but it might be nice if she hears that from you too," said Mom, as she reached for a glass of champagne.

"I'll be sure to talk to her," said Aunt Christine. "I promise."

"Look, I know Mom can seem tough and indifferent at times, but she's really not," smiled Mom wanly. "And even though she likes to pretend that she's invincible, she's not immune to the worries and fears that every mother carries deep within their heart." She took a sip of champagne and then added, "Anyway, the point I'm trying to make is that she loves you more than you'll ever know, and the idea of losing you to Nancy, with all of her wealth and prestige, is something that truly terrifies her."

"Oh, my God, I had no idea she felt that way," said Aunt Christine. "I've never known her to think that way about anything. She's always been so confident and self-assured."

"Well, you're not just anything, Chrissy," said Mom. "You're her baby girl, so maybe try taking it a little bit easier on her, okay?"

"Yes, of course," she nodded.

"Hey, go have fun," encouraged Mom. "This is your special weekend, and you need to enjoy it."

Before Aunt Christine had a chance to respond, Nancy walked over to us.

"Christine, I think your bridesmaids are getting a little out of control," she said testily. "Would you please go and tell them to quiet down? Believe it or not, we do have neighbors who enjoy the solitude of this neighborhood."

"Oh, I'm so sorry," said Aunt Christine. "I'll go and talk to them right now."

Watching the two of them walk away, Mom curled her lip and said, "You're Grandmother's right, she is a colossal bitch."

Chapter Twenty-Three

The next afternoon brought high spirits and elation as we laughed, chatted, and drank mimosas in the sun-drenched expanse of the Laurel Estates bridal suite. It was a beautiful room designed to make every bride feel like royalty, with gilded mirrors lining each wall, plush, ivory sofas, and luxurious chaise lounges scattered throughout.

Aunt Christine looked absolutely radiant as she stepped away from the hair and makeup area and over to where her wedding dress was hanging. As she went to reach for it, a sudden, merciless hot flash surged right through her, painting her cheeks a fiery red and sending beads of sweat directly across her forehead and upper lip, making it look as if her face was slathered with Vaseline. It was both relentless and unstoppable, and just as her panic was about to set in, Mom swept into action and went in search of a fan to help cool her down.

"Oh my God, where is she?" asked Aunt Christine, rapidly fanning herself. "My makeup is about to melt off."

"Your makeup is just fine, sweetie," said Crystal. "The setting spray we used is going to keep it from sweating off, so you don't need to worry about that."

"Here, why don't you have another mimosa?" said Polly, handing her a glass. "I'm sure she'll be back any minute."

"She's already been gone five minutes," whimpered Aunt Christine. "What if she can't find one?"

"She'll find one," I smiled reassuringly. "Mom is nothing if not resourceful."

"I'm here!" exclaimed Mom, running into the room. "Crisis averted, I found one!" She quickly plugged in the rotating fan and placed it in front of Aunt Christine. "You just need to stay calm and let the air cool you down."

"Ugh, I can't believe I'm having such a bad hot flash," said Aunt Christine irritably. "And on my wedding day, no less!" She closed her eyes in frustration and yelled out. "I don't have time for this! I need to get into my wedding dress!"

"Honey, we'll get you into your wedding dress," said Michelle. "Don't you worry."

"Not if I don't stop sweating, you won't," countered Aunt Christine. She stared into the mirror worriedly. "Is my makeup okay? I don't have time to redo it."

"Your makeup is fine," reassured Mom. "But the sooner you calm down, the sooner this hot flash is going to stop. You're not helping matters by freaking out, so just take a deep breath and try to relax, okay?"

"Okay," she nodded.

Michelle handed her a glass of ice water. "Here, drink this. It should help you cool down some."

"Thank you," she smiled wanly.

As Aunt Christine was drinking the water, Grandma Helen walked into the room.

"Well, everyone is beginning to arrive, and the stage is now set," she said, sashaying into the room. She walked over to where Mom was holding the fan in front of Aunt Christine. "My God, what's happening to you? Have you been running laps or something?"

"What do you think's happening to her, Mother?" said Mom. "She's having a hot flash."

"You're still having those?" she asked. "I thought you were well past all that."

"I'm only 47, Mother," said Aunt Christine irritably. "So, no, I'm still dealing with them."

"Well, you're going to need to get over it quickly, dear," she said dismissively. "We have ten minutes to get you into that dress and down that aisle."

"That's going to help her stress levels, Mother. Thank you," said Mom.

"Ugh, why won't this stop?" bellowed Aunt Christine. "I can't let everyone see me like this."

"Close your eyes and take deep breaths," said Mom. "You're stressing over this is making things worse."

"Your sister's right, darling," agreed Grandma Helen, patting her hand. "You just need to relax." She looked over at Polly, Michelle, and Crystal. "Girls, would you mind gathering up the rest of the bridal party so that everyone is ready once Christine comes out?"

"Yes, of course," smiled Polly, walking over to the door. "Are you sure you don't need one of us to stay behind and help?"

"That won't be necessary, dear," she smiled. "Olivia, Addie, and I can manage the rest."

Grandma Helen watched the three of them walk out the door and turned back to Aunt Christine.

"Now, where were we?" she wondered aloud. "Oh, yes, hot flash!" She placed her hands on Aunt Christine's shoulders and began to massage them. "Your father would always do this for me whenever they got really bad. I found that they went away rather quickly when I just let go and stopped fighting them."

"Thank you, Mom," she smiled gratefully.

Mom and I watched quietly as Aunt Christine placed her hand softly atop Grandma Helen's.

"I hope you know how much I Iove you," she said quietly. "And I hope you know that you are incredibly important to me, and always will be. Yes, we banter back and forth and make jokes at each other's expense, but that's only because we know that our relationship is strong enough to withstand it."

She stood to face Grandma Helen.

"I am the woman I am today because of you, Mom," she continued. "You taught me about life, love, and how to be accepting of who I am. You encouraged me to take chances and follow my dreams, and it's because of you that I have lived a full life with absolutely no regrets. I attribute a lot of who I am to you, and I need you to know that you will always be an important part of my life. Nancy will never be able to live up to any of that, and her money means absolutely nothing to me. Being your daughter and knowing that you will always be there for me is what matters. It's all that's ever mattered. So please don't worry about Nancy. She is not my mother, you are. And for that, I will be forever grateful."

"Oh, darling, I love you too," she cried, wiping her eyes. "I was just so afraid I was going to lose you."

"You are never going to lose me," said Aunt Christine pointedly. "That, I can promise you."

"Even though that vile, Carpenters-loving, Neil Diamond-hating, wretch of a woman bought you a house?" she sniffed.

"Yes," she laughed. "Even though she bought us a house."

"See, I told you that you had nothing to worry about," said Mom, putting her arm around Grandma Helen. "Nancy will never be able to take the place of you, and no one else can either, for that matter. You are definitely one of a kind."

"On that, we can all agree," smiled Grandma Helen contentedly. She looked up at the clock hanging on the wall. "Oh, my God, we're going to be late! Christine, you have got to get dressed right now."

She hurried over to the door. "I'll keep everyone preoccupied by making my appearance. I'm sure they're all wondering what I'm wearing. I am the mother of the bride after all."

And with that, she walked out the door.

"Yeah, definitely one of a kind, that one," agreed Aunt Christine.

"Delusional is more like it," said Mom, unzipping Aunt Christine's garment bag. "She may think she's the opening act, but you're the main event." She held up the dress and smiled excitedly. "Come on, let's get you ready for your grand entrance."

***

As I stood beside Mom, bouquet clasped tightly in my hands, I could feel the hush of anticipation ripple through the garden. Every guest seemed to lean into the moment, their quiet excitement building as they waited for the ceremony to begin. Then, just as the music swelled, Aunt Christine appeared. She stepped into view with a calm, radiant smile, her arm gently linked with Grandpa Anthony's. His pace was slow, steady, and deliberate. Each step measured, as though he were trying to hold onto the moment just a little longer. His face remained composed, almost stoic, but his eyes told another story entirely. They shimmered with emotion, a tender blend of pride and nostalgia, as if he were seeing not just the woman beside him, but every version of the little girl she had once been.

As Aunt Christine and Grandpa Anthony continued their slow walk down the aisle, I found my gaze drifting over to Brian. There was something almost reverent in the way he looked at her. Every emotion was laid bare. Love, awe, and complete adoration. It lived openly in his expression and in the way his gaze never wavered. The love he felt for her wasn't subtle or fleeting. It was steadfast, sacred, and undeniable, and I found myself praying that I, too, might find a love like that someday.

When they reached the altar, Grandpa Anthony carefully took Aunt Christine's hand and placed it into Brian's, his grip lingering, warm and reluctant, as though he were holding onto one last fleeting moment with his little girl. Then, with a quiet, knowing nod, he released her and stepped back to take a seat next to Grandma Helen.

Clearing his throat, the preacher began the ceremony.

"Dearly beloved," he began, his voice rich and steady. "We are gathered here today, in the presence of God, to witness and bless the union of Christine and Brian in holy matrimony."

Opening his Bible, he began to read aloud.

"Scripture tells us in 1 Corinthians that 'love is patient, love is kind. That bears all things, believes all things, hopes all things, endures all things.' This kind of love is not simply felt, it is lived. It is given to us by God, and it calls on each and every one of us to reflect Him in the way we love one another." He closed the book softly. "Today, you have chosen to make a covenant, not only with each other, but with God Himself, and in that covenant, you have also chosen to write your own vows. Words that have come from prayer, reflection, and from the work God has already begun in both of your hearts."

He paused momentarily and looked over at Brian.

Brian, you may begin," he smiled softly.

Turning to face Aunt Christine, Brian gently reached for her hands.

"Christine," he began, his voice steady but soft. "Today, I stand here grateful. Grateful for you, for the love we share, and for the life we've only just begun to imagine. I promise to love you with patience, with honesty, and with the kind of devotion that doesn't waver, even when life gets hard. I vow to support your dreams, to lift you when you stumble, and to stand beside you through every season, whether they are easy or difficult.

I promise to be your partner in all things: to laugh with you, to grow with you, to face whatever comes our way, together. I will choose you every day. In the quiet moments, in the ordinary moments, and in the moments that seem too small to even matter. You are my best friend, my home, and my heart, and I promise, from this day forward, to spend every day proving that you are the person I want beside me for all the days of my life."

Aunt Christine, blinking away tears, began to recite her own vows.

"Brian," she said, a soft smile lighting her face. "I thank God every day for you, and for the love we share. I promise to stand beside you, not just as your partner, but as your best friend. I will support you, encourage you, and walk with you through whatever life brings our way. I vow to laugh with you, dream with you, build a life with you, and grow old with you. Through every high and low, every joy and trial, I promise to hold your hand and never let go. And regardless of what the years may bring, or how the world changes, I promise to always choose you, our life, and our love every day for the rest of my life."

Seeing that she had finished, the preacher stepped forward.

"What you have spoken here today reflects not only your love for one another, but also your faith in the One who brought you together." He lifted his gaze, taking in the faces of everyone present. "Let us pray."

Bowing his head and closing his eyes, he continued. "Father, we thank You for this blessed union of Christine and Brian. We ask that You pour Your grace over this marriage, and over the families who surround them with love and support. Strengthen their bond in times of trial, deepen it in times of joy, and keep it firmly anchored in Your truth. May their home be a place of peace, of kindness, and full of Your abiding presence. We ask for this in Jesus' name, Amen."

"Amen," the room echoed softly.

Looking once more at Brian and Aunt Christine, he said. "Having made these vows before God and these witnesses, and by the authority granted in me, I now pronounce you husband and wife. What God has joined together, let no one separate." A gentle smile crossed his face as he winked at Brian. "You may now kiss your bride."

Chapter Twenty-Four

The reception was held in a beautifully refurbished barn on the southern stretch of Laurel Estates, no more than a short walk from the garden where the ceremony had taken place. As we stepped inside, we could see that the entire space had been magnificently dressed in the colors of early autumn. Round tables draped in deep ivory and burlap-toned linens filled the room, their softened textures easing the barn's rustic edges. At the center of each, lush arrangements of sunflowers, rust-colored dahlias, and burnt orange roses gathered in warm, abundant clusters, lending a quiet richness to the naturally unadorned space. Throughout the room there were white candles flickering softly in amber glass holders, their honeyed light settling gently over everything it touched, drawing the room inward and softening its breadth, making it feel warm and intimate.

"Oh, my God, this is absolutely exquisite!" gasped Mom, as she glanced around the room. "Between the ceremony ornamentation and all of this, I'm completely in awe. You have truly outdone yourself, Christian."

"It really is stunning," I agreed. "I can't believe the transformation."

"Well, it doesn't hurt that Christine has great taste," he smiled. "Although I must admit, it is rather spectacular." He leaned in closely and lowered his voice. "But it certainly wasn't without a struggle, that's for sure."

"What do you mean?" asked Mom.

"Well, Nancy and I had a bit of a disagreement about the floral arrangements," he said. "She wanted me to add water lilies and carnations since those are Christine and Brian's birth flowers, but I adamantly said no." He gestured toward one of the tables. "I mean, can you imagine the atrocity if I had allowed that? My reputation would have been ruined. Those flowers have absolutely no place in a fall bouquet!"

"That's an odd request," said Mom.

"Yes, well, she's a bit of an odd woman, so I suppose it makes sense." He folded his arms and chuckled. "Carnations and water lilies. Uh, not on my watch."

As we stood laughing about the near desecration of Christian's autumnal floral bouquet, I noticed a young woman waving frantically at him, trying to get his attention.

"Um, I think that girl over there needs you," I said.

"Ugh, this can't be good," he sighed irritably. "Miriam knows not to bother me unless it's an emergency." He nodded in her direction before smiling over at us. "Well, let's hope it's not too much of a catastrophe."

As soon as Christian walked away, Beau came over and stood next to Mom.

"I am so glad that the ceremony is finally over with," he said. "I honestly thought we were never going to make it out of there."

"What are you talking about?" asked Mom. "It took less than twenty minutes from start to finish."

"Which is fifteen minutes too long, if you ask me," he countered. "Just say 'I do,' exchange your rings, and be done with it. Most people are only here for the reception, anyway."

"Not much of a romantic, are you?" drawled Mom, raising her brow.

"Nah, I consider myself more of a realist," he said. "I find it to be much more grounding."

"Well, good luck explaining that to your future wife," said Mom.

"Luck won't be needed," he said confidently. "The girl I marry is going to be so completely enamored with me that she'll do whatever I say."

"That's a bold statement for someone who knows absolutely nothing about women," she said, putting her arm around him. "However, in time, I think you may find that your views on the matter will—"

"Oh, sweet, is that prime rib?" he interrupted, his attention shifting to a chef slicing into a large standing rib roast. "I'm starving!"

We watched as he darted over to the other side of the room and grabbed a plate.

"That poor child hasn't a clue, has he?" sighed Mom.

"Mom, a brain-eating bacteria would literally starve in that boy's head," I said. "He's not the sharpest tool in the shed."

"That's not true," she said. "He's actually incredibly smart. He just tends to overlook reality sometimes, that's all."

Looking across the room, she could see that Brian and Christine were talking with Grandma Helen and Grandpa Anthony.

"Come on," she said. "Let's go see what they're talking about."

As we began making our way over to where they were standing, we were intercepted by Nana and Pops, who, by the look of things, had been taking full advantage of the open bar.

"Oh, Olivia, this place looks absolutely amazing!" exclaimed Nana. "And I'm just in love with all the fall colors. It's as if the beauty of the season made its way indoors."

"Thank you, Carol, but I can't take any credit," smiled Mom. "This is all Christian's doing. He had the vision, and he's the one who made it happen."

"Well, please be sure to tell him that I think he's incredibly talented," she said. "Oh, and also let him know that the bartender is making the best Blue Hawaiians with the cutest little umbrellas in them." She lifted her glass. "Isn't it adorable?"

"How many of those have you had, Nana?" I asked.

"Oh, I don't know," she shrugged. "Maybe two?"

"You've had three," said Pops. "And before you think about having another, you're going to have something to eat."

"Oh, that's right, we do need to eat, don't we?" she giggled. "I guess I've just been having so much fun, I forgot."

"Do you need any help, George?" asked Mom, quietly pulling Pop's aside.

"Nah, I think I can wrangle this one by myself," he winked. He placed a hand on Nana's back and steered toward the buffet. "Come on, honey, let's go make you a plate."

"And then we can get another Blue Hawaiian!" she said excitedly.

"Let's just see how you're feeling, okay?" he smiled.

"Good Lord, that man is going to have his hands full tonight," said Mom, watching them walk away. "Please remind me to tell your father that his mother is doubling down on Blue Hawaiians, and that Pop's may need some help with her later."

By the time we made our way over to Grandma Helen and Grandpa Anthony, Aunt Christine and Brian had left to go over to the other side of the room.

"Olivia, darling, your father and I have been discussing that adorable little wine place we went to up in Ball Ground," said Grandma Helen. "And I think we'd like to join you and Gregory there next weekend. How does that sound?"

"Yes, of course," smiled Mom. "I'm sure we could do that."

"And, of course, I had to tell him all about that darling little bald man who knows about the different wines and where they're from," continued Grandma Helen. "You know, the one who looks like Stanley Tucci?"

"Yes, Mother, I know who he is," said Mom.

"I believe they call those people sommeliers, dear," said Grandpa Anthony.

"Yes, that," nodded Grandma Helen in agreement. "Anyway, I was telling him that the two of them are sure to get along famously, since you know, they both know so much about wine."

"He may be very busy with his other patrons, Helen, so he may not have a lot of time to spend with us," said Grandpa Anthony. "But I'm very interested in meeting him."

Oh, don't be silly, Anthony," she said, with the wave of her hand. "The man loves about talking wine. He won't have any problem spending time with people who understand it too."

Grandma Helen clapped her hands together excitedly. "Oh, and then I thought we'd go over to that adorable little Schnitzel place for lunch."

"It's a German butcher, Mother, but yes, we can certainly do that as well," corrected Mom.

"Hey, beautiful," said Dad, kissing Mom on the cheek. "I was just about to get something to eat. Would you care to join me?"

"You know, why don't we all get something to eat?" suggested Grandma Helen. "And then we can fill Gregory in on next weekend's plans."

"Uh, next weekend?" he said, looking confused.

"We're going to drink wine and dine on Bavarian cuisine, dear," said Grandma Helen jovially. "And then, I suppose, we'll just have to see where the wind takes us."

"Oh, okay," said Dad, a bit uneasily. "That sounds both fun and ominous."

***

Once everyone had finished eating and the dinner plates were cleared, the DJ quickly quieted down the music to make an announcement.

"Ladies and gentlemen, if I could just have your attention for a moment."

He waited for all of the guests to settle down before continuing.

"On behalf of Brian and Christine, I extend their deepest gratitude to each of you for being here tonight. Words fall short of capturing how truly honored they feel to be surrounded by so many familiar and cherished faces. To share this moment with all of you is not only meaningful, but a profound and wonderful blessing."

A faint smile touched his lips as he glanced across the room to where Brian and Aunt Christine were standing.

"And now, please join me in inviting Mr. and Mrs. Brian Caldwell up to the dance floor for their first dance together as husband and wife."

The room erupted in raucous applause as Brian and Aunt Christine made their way to the dance floor. Many guests had already begun forming a circle around the dance floor, lifting their phones to capture this momentous moment. As soon as the two of them stepped to the center of the dance floor, Brian gently placed his hand on Aunt Christine's waist. I watched her look up at him with adoration and silently mouth the words, 'I love you,' just as the beginning notes of *At Last* by Etta James began to play.

"You know, I don't think I've ever seen your sister so happy," smiled Grandma Helen. She gently reached for Mom's hand and smiled serenely. "I just know she's found her perfect match in Brian, just like you found your perfect match in Gregory."

"Well, considering he's now a member of this crazy family, he's going to have to be," mumbled Dad.

"Shut up," whispered Mom, giving him the side-eye.

"Oh, those two look so in love," cooed Nana, as she and Pops stepped beside us. "And they make such a handsome couple, too. I suppose it's too late for them to have children, isn't it?"

"Considering they're both in their late forties, dear, I would say so," said Grandma Helen.

As Brian and Aunt Christine continued their dance, Grandma Helen began motioning for the DJ to wrap it up.

"Oh, my God, don't you dare," warned Mom.

"Don't I dare do what?" she asked innocently.

"Don't you dare try getting that man to rush their first dance, Mother," said Mom. "Christine will never forgive you, and neither will I."

"I'm not trying to rush him, darling," she said. "I'm simply letting him know that it's time for the parents of the bride to join them."

"Yes, when their dance is finished," said Mom. "And, as you can plainly see, it's not."

Grandma Helen watched as Nancy and Tim began making their way through the crowd.

"Ugh, they're still here," she sneered. "I was rather hoping someone locked them in the back freezer."

"They're the parents of the groom, Mother, so you may as well accept that you're going to have to share the limelight with them," said Mom. "It's Brian's wedding too."

"True," nodded Grandma Helen. "But at least your father and I will be introduced first. I made sure of that."

"What do you mean you made sure of that?" asked Mom.

"Oh, I just made sure to tell the DJ that Christine had asked for your father and me to join them on the dance floor before Tim and Nancy, that's all," she shrugged.

"You did what?" hissed Mom.

"Oh, calm down, Olivia," she scoffed. "I simply explained that it's tradition in our family for the bride's parents to dance first."

"What are you talking about?" said Mom. "That's never been a tradition in our family."

"Yes, I know that," she smiled. "But he doesn't. I even wrote it down so that he doesn't forget."

Just as Brian and Aunt Christine's dance was beginning to wind down, Grandma Helen spotted Nancy zeroing in on a white sheet of paper hanging in the DJ's booth, like it had personally offended her. Picking it up, she quickly read it over, and shook her head in immediate disapproval. She then had a short and curt discussion with the DJ, who nodded his head in understanding before promptly grabbing a pen to cross out what had been written on the note.

"That bitch!" hissed Grandma Helen under her breath. "She did not just do that."

"Do what?" asked Mom. "What happened?"

Before Grandma Helen could answer, the DJ lifted his microphone. "Alright, folks, now it's time for the parents of both Brian and Christine to come and join them out on the dance floor." Watching the two couples make their way to the center of the room, he then added excitedly, "Make sure to come in close because this is a moment for you to celebrate together. Two families becoming one, surrounded by love, family, and friends!"

The look on Grandma Helen's face said it all.

"Is she okay?" I asked.

"Yeah, she's fine," said Mom. "She's just experiencing what many of us know as karma."

Chapter Twenty-five

Oh, dear God, that was simply dreadful," shuddered Grandma Helen. "The very mention of our two families becoming one practically made me ill. I have no need, nor desire, to be reminded that those godawful people are now tied to us. Thank God Brian is nothing like them."

"Well, Tim doesn't seem to be too bad," said Mom. "I actually kind of like him."

"Yes, well, knowing he's tied to Nancy is enough to make me avoid them both," she sneered. "How he and Brian have the patience to put up with her, I will never fully understand."

From across the room, we could see Nancy scowling at us as she made her way over to where we were standing.

"Oh, great, the witch is on her broom and headed straight for us," growled Grandma Helen. "Why can't she just leave us alone?"

"Please try to be nice, Mother," said Mom. "After the reception you won't have to deal with her anymore."

"From your lips to God's ears, darling," she sighed. "Because I am running out of patience with her."

"Helen, there you are," said Nancy, sidling up next to her. "I wanted to tell you about the strangest thing that I saw hanging in the DJ's booth. It was a note saying that you and Anthony were to join Brian and Christine on the dance floor before Tim and me. Of course, I figured that it had to be some sort of miscommunication, so I quickly made the necessary correction, but still, who does that?"

"As you said, I'm sure it was some sort of miscommunication," answered Grandma Helen civilly.

"Was it?" snapped Nancy, raising her brow.

"Yes," replied Grandma Helen coolly.

"Somehow I doubt that," scoffed Nancy, crossing her arms angrily. "I know you think you're some sort of belle of the ball or something, but that's nothing but a delusion. You are nowhere near as important as you think you are, and it's time someone tells you that. You're nothing but an old, washed-up has-been who gets her kicks out of doing elderly community theater. It's actually pretty pathetic."

"Now wait just one minute," said Mom, moving in between them. "I don't know who you think you are, Nancy, but you have absolutely no right to talk to my mother that way. And, if I'm being honest, you're one to talk. You're a morose and miserable person who does everything in your power to belittle those around you. You did it the very first night we met and have continued to do it every single time, since." She took a deep breath, and then added, "Now, I'm certainly not saying that my mother is innocent in any of this—"

"Olivia!" interrupted Grandma Helen indignantly.

"Mother, it's true," said Mom, quieting her down. "You know it, I know, and so does everyone else. So stop acting like you're blameless."

Mom looked back over at Nancy. "But you and your snarky attitude at the rehearsal dinner last night were completely unacceptable. Not because of what you and Tim gifted to Brian and Christine, but the way in which you chose to go about it. You were smug, rude, and did everything you could to rub her nose in it."

"Oh, please," began Nancy dismissively. "She would have done the exact same thing."

"Actually, no, dear, I wouldn't have," replied Grandma Helen. "I may be obstinate, uncooperative, and demanding, but I would never knowingly parade my wealth around in such an ostentatious and boastful manner. Even I have standards."

"How dare you!" she hissed.

"Uh, hello, everyone," came a deep voice behind a microphone. "May I have your attention, please?"

We immediately stopped our quarreling and turned our attention to the center of the dance floor.

"Um, I hope you don't mind, but I thought it'd be fun to do a little impromptu sing-along with my favorite duet partner," smiled Brian.

"Excuse me, but my son needs me," said Nancy pompously, turning to make her way over to him. But what he said next made her stop cold in her tracks.

"Helen, would you do me the honor of singing our song with me?" he beamed brightly, holding out a second microphone. "I think you know the one I'm talking about."

"Of course, my darling!" she exclaimed, taking the microphone. "And I want you to know that the honor is mine, dear."

Had I not just witnessed Nancy's denigration of Grandma Helen minutes ago, I would have actually felt sorry for her. The utter contempt and disdain that were evident on her face not thirty seconds ago was now replaced with sadness and humiliation as she watched Grandma Helen take her place next to Brian.

As the first notes of *Islands in the Stream* began to play, Brian lovingly put his arm around Grandma Helen and spoke softly into the microphone.

"You know you'll always be the Dolly to my Kenny, Helen," he winked.

Swaying back and forth, they began to sing in unison.

"Islands in the stream
That is what we are
No one in between
How can we be wrong
Sail away with me
To another world
And we rely on each other, ah-ah
From one lover to another, ah-ah."

"Oh my God, don't they look absolutely adorable?" said Aunt Christine, walking up to us. "Brian wanted to make it a surprise. It killed me not to say anything."

"Yeah, well, I don't think she's the only one who's surprised," said Mom, nodding in Nancy's direction.

"Oh, she'll get over it," said Aunt Christine. "She's not much of a singer anyway. Brian says she sounds like a cat in heat, so by keeping her away from the microphone, we're actually doing the world a favor."

"It was sweet of him to think of her," said Mom. "She's had a rough couple of days."

"I know she has," said Aunt Christine. "But performing has always had a therapeutic effect on her, so I think she's going to be just fine."

As soon as Brian and Grandma Helen finished their duet, the dance floor came alive, immediately filling with guests eager to celebrate. Polly and Michelle eventually found themselves having to babysit Crystal, whose growing intoxication and increasingly indiscreet affection kept them in a constant state of quiet intervention. Ezra and Sabrina, on the other hand, kept themselves curiously insulated from the rising tide of music and laughter as they danced slowly together, completely unaware of anything else around them.

Grandma Helen and Grandpa Anthony spent the evening in easy conversation with a handful of familiar couples, while Tim and Nancy mirrored their actions and did the same thing on the opposite side of the room. As for Mom and Dad, they moved effortlessly through the night, laughing and dancing in a way that I hadn't seen before. After 25 years of marriage, the two of them looked more in love than ever, and it completely warmed my heart.

And threading through it all was Beau, staying just out of sight as he steadily filled small, illicit to-go containers with anything he could quietly salvage. It was a careful and practiced kind of thievery, and one that immediately came to a halt the minute our mother caught him trying to abscond with half of the wedding cake.

As for me, I sat back and watched it all. Life was good at the moment, and I wanted to relish it. College was going incredibly well for me, and I was surprised at how quickly I was able to acclimate. Living at home and not having to play soccer was more rewarding than I had originally thought. Not to mention, I get a front row seat to Mom driving Beau crazy with all of his eighth-grade coursework.

I was currently pondering this very thought when the DJ made an announcement for all single ladies to make their way out on the dance floor for the throwing of the bouquet.

"Aren't you going out there?" asked Mom.

"Are you kidding?" I said. "Have you even seen the grit and determination on Crystal's face? Someone's going to get hurt out there."

We quietly watched as Aunt Christine tossed her wedding bouquet into the small crowd of women standing behind her. As predicted,

Crystal immediately shoved at least four of them out of her way as she dived forward to catch it. However, at the last minute, it tumbled out of her hands and landed directly in front of Polly, who swiftly picked it up and grinned triumphantly as she waved it in the air.

"I tell you, that girl has absolutely no couth," said Grandma Helen, shaking her head. "She looks so desperate and hopeless. It's sad, really."

"Ladies and gentlemen, if you will please take a moment to line up outside, Brian and Christine will be heading that way very soon," said the DJ. "Oh, and please be sure to pick up a satchel of rose petals on your way out. That way they're sure to get a colorful sendoff."

Our entire family had grouped together as we waved goodbye to Brian and Aunt Christine. Rose petals littered their path as they ran hand-in-hand toward their limo. They looked happier than I had ever seen them, and I was so excited for the future to come.

As soon as the limo pulled away, Mom, Grandma Helen, and I turned and followed everyone back into the reception hall.

"You know, dear," said Grandma Helen, crossing over the threshold. "I really appreciate you defending me earlier with Nancy."

"Well, she shouldn't have come at you like that," said Mom. "It was completely uncalled for. Also, I could see that it was starting to get to you, and I didn't want you to say or do something that would make it worse."

"I wasn't about to ruin Christine's wedding with petty quarreling," said Grandma Helen, shaking her head. "I like to think I'm better than that."

"Well, just know that I'm really proud of you," smiled Mom. "I know that wasn't easy."

"Thank you, dear," she said, patting Mom's hand. "I really would like to work on being a more tolerant and empathetic person."

Suddenly, a scream erupted from across the room as Nancy jumped out of her seat to berate a server who had just spilled a full glass of water in her lap.

"But, then again, maybe I should start that tomorrow," she winked.

"Oh, my God, Mother, you didn't," whispered Mom in horror. "Please tell me you didn't orchestrate that."

"Of course, not, darling," she scoffed. "I would never do something like that to someone."

Wearing a grin that was sly and unmistakably pleased with itself, she drew in a deep breath and said, "Now, how about we have that adorable little bartender mix us up a round of Helentinis?"

The End.

A Letter From Tiffany

Thank you so much for reading *Tailored and Veiled: A Delightfully Dysfunctional Familial Wedding,* the fourth installment in the Delightfully Dysfunctional series. I hope you had as much fun reading it as I had writing it. If you haven't already, please be sure to check out the first three books in the series, *Crazed and Confused, Jingled and Jangled, and Traveled and Unraveled.* The Jenkins are very near and dear to my heart, so you can rest assured that I have quite a few more books planned for the series.

I always love hearing from my readers, so please feel free to drop me a message anytime via Facebook, Instagram, and/or my personal website. My interaction with you is what motivates me to write, so please reach out anytime. Facebook and Instagram are where I share information on new and upcoming books, major announcements, book signings, etc., so please be sure to follow me there so that you can stay informed and up to date on things.

Facebook Page: https://www.facebook.com/TiffanyRyanAuthor

Instagram Page: https://www.instagram.com/tiffany_ryan_author

Website: tiffanyryanwrites.com

Sincerely,
Tiffany

Acknowledgements

I often say this, but it takes a group of talented and selfless individuals to help any Indie Author publish a book. Thankfully, God has placed a few amazing individuals in my corner, and for that, I will be eternally grateful.

First and foremost, I would like to thank Tambi Smith, who has continually and selflessly given so much of her time and talent to help me bring the Jenkins family to life. She is my sounding board, editor, and one of my greatest friends. Thank you for being my rock, Tambi. You have no idea how much I appreciate all that you do.

I would also like to thank Darin Miller, who is not only one of my best author friends, but also someone who has given selflessly of his time to act as a second editor. If you're not familiar with his book series, The Dwayne Morrow Mysteries, then you need to be. It is one of my favorite series, and he, of course, has become one of my favorite authors.

To my mother, Kathleen Catalano, thank you for always being my greatest cheerleader and biggest supporter. Your unwavering commitment to tell everyone and their mother about me and my books is probably what keeps me in business. Thank you for always having my back.

Gabriel and Mckenna, there would be no Jenkins family if it weren't for you. Thank you for the endless material you provide daily. I suppose I owe you both royalties, but for now, my love will have to suffice.

Lastly, I would like to thank my husband, Blake, for always having faith in me. You're the life that breathes in me, and I thank God daily for bringing you into my life. I love you.

www.ingramcontent.com/pod-product-compliance
Lightning Source LLC
La Vergne TN
LVHW010700110826
845149LV00014B/3176

* 9 7 9 8 9 8 8 6 9 8 3 7 1 *